Converso

Mario X. Martinez

Converso

Gaon Books
www.gaonbooks.com

Manufactured in the United States of America

Library of Congress Cataloging-in-Publication Data

Martinez, Mario X., 1952-
  Converso / Mario X. Martinez.
    p. cm. -- (Western Sephardim and Crypto-Jews; v. 3)
  ISBN 978-0-9820657-7-8
  1. Jews--New Mexico--Fiction. 2. Crypto Jews--Fiction.
3. Identification (Religion)--Fiction. 4. New Mexico--History--
19th century--Fiction. I. Title.

  PS3613.A78646C66 2009
  813'.6--dc22
                                        2009015314
British Cataloguing-in-Publication data for this book is available
from the British Library.

Cover Art

The cover image by Gloria Abella Ballen focuses on the
junxtaposition of Judaism and Christianity in the crypto-
Jewish experience. The image is composed of a *yad* (hand-like
Torah scroll pointer) on the left with a sacred Hebrew text
and on the right an arm pointing toward heaven amidst the
baroque columns of a Spanish church.

Contents

Series

Western Sephardic Traditions

Isabelle Medina-Sandoval, Editor

Gaon Books about Western Sephardic life and history
from Europe to the Americas, exploring experiences from
the Diaspora, including crypto-Judaism.

Volume I
*Cantos judeo-españoles:
simbología poética y visión del mundo*
Silvia Hamui Sutton

Volume II
Guardians of Hidden Traditions,
Isabelle Medina-Sandoval

Volume III
Converso,
Mario X. Martinez

Dedication

to my
Father and Mother

Jacobo Domingo and Ana Maria (Valencia) Martinez

September 23, 1950

A special thanks to my Grand Inquisitor, Alice, for her
countless hours of editing assistance.

Prologue

My maternal grandmother was a remarkable woman who raised not only several of her younger siblings after her mother died unexpectedly, but six of her own children after being widowed in her early 40's. She possessed a caring spirit and an amazing memory. Being the eldest of her 20 grandchildren and her baptismal godson, I was accorded a special status and was the lucky recipient of her delightful, and sometimes sad, recollections of her life. Through her oral history, I got to know her parents, siblings, and relatives who had played a part in her life while growing up in Rio Sagrado, New Mexico.

Sometime around my thirteenth birthday, my grandmother shared perhaps her most startling tale with me. Thankfully, this took place before her health declined and her mind was ravaged by dementia. I couldn't help but notice as her blue eyes cast a furtive glance toward the front door before she spoke in the familiar combination of Spanish and English favored by many of her contemporaries. My *abuela* proceeded to tell me a story about the Sephardim, the Jews of Spain, who lost their homeland and struggled to find new homes in faraway lands. Persecution followed them wherever they journeyed. Out of necessity, they concealed their religious identity and adapted to the predominant order. Some even tried to abandon their old practices.

This is a story of a perilous discovery that was made during a time of joy and prosperity by my grandmother's parents, Abran and Isabella Espinosa.

Chapter One

Rio Sagrado, New Mexico Territory - 1879. Like many of the smaller communities surrounding Santa Fe, the religious needs of this village had been neglected for as long as anyone could remember. The promise of a parish priest by the Bishop of Durango in 1833 never materialized during the Mexican rule. The few priests that journeyed north to the more affluent towns found that their support was dependent on the subsistence farming and limited resources. The harsh reality of frontier life dictated that the welfare of the priests, as well as the churches in their custody, was left wanting.

Strangely enough, the advent of the American occupation in 1846 would eventually lead to a spiritual renewal. Five years after General Stephen Watts Kearney claimed New Mexico for the United States and one year after it became a territory, Jean Baptiste Lamy arrived in Santa Fe in 1851 to assume leadership of the Catholic Church. Two years later, his appointment as Bishop of Santa Fe concurred with New Mexico's removal from the Diocese of Durango's jurisdiction.

Forty-plus churches would be built under Lamy's administration in the ensuing decades. He recruited many priests from outside of New Mexico, including French priests, to minister to these new parishes. In the fall of 1877, a delegation from Rio Sagrado, led by *Don* Pablo Espinosa, journeyed to Santa Fe to confer with Lamy, who had since been elevated to Archbishop, to present their proposal for a church to be named after San Ysidro, the patron saint of farmers. The largest portion of the funding would be underwritten by *Don* Pablo.

The amount of their financial support and their fervor impressed the Archbishop, who approved the project without hesitation. Construction on the church started as soon as the delegation returned to Rio Sagrado.

Months later, the inhabitants of Rio Sagrado and its neighboring communities were gathered on a radiant spring morning to celebrate one of the most memorable days of their lives. A religious procession made its way through a gauntlet of solemn villagers led by Archbishop Lamy, now a sixty-six year-old man of short, frail stature. Father Pierre LaSalle dutifully trailed his superior by two paces. The lanky thirty year-old man with classic Gallic features appeared somewhat detached from the celebration compared to the Archbishop, who cheerfully blessed the devout villagers every few seconds.

Several middle-age dignitaries were preceded by six musicians; four of them were playing guitars of various sizes while two were playing fiddles. One could see from the well-attired group's comportment and European lineament, that they were esteemed members of the community. The men were wearing formal black coats and vests, starched white linen shirts, and black wool pants while their spouses proudly wore their ornately-trimmed silk dresses, matching *mantillas*, and fans purchased especially for this auspicious occasion. The procession approached a festively-decorated clearing in front of the new church.

Three young people watched intently from the edge of the clearing, their striking features and fair complexions set them apart from the others around them. Isabella Lucero, a shapely 18 year-old woman-child with auburn hair and green eyes, stood on the left side. Beside her is Abran Espinosa, a handsome 21 year-old male possessing a medium build and a youthful, sometimes brash, exuberance. Clemente Valencia, a similar-aged muscular male, flanked his cousin Abran. He was Abran's partner in crime and a dependable, loyal friend of Abran and Isabella.

Isabella could hardly contain herself while clutching her hands to her breast, "Isn't this so wonderful? Where did all these people come from?"

"From all around the valley I guess," replied Abran.

He turned to Clemente and winked impishly. "What do you think, Cleme?"

"*Pues*, I recognize many faces. They probably came here out of boredom." Clemente wrinkled his nose and pointed with his chin into the crowd, "Even those goat herders from Cañoncito made it here."

"I think all these people came to eat our tasty food and get drunk with the Archbishop, *¿qué no?*" mocked Abran.

The two males struggled to stifle their laughter while Isabella nudged Abran with her elbow. She noticed the disapproving glances from the nearby adults and blushed, "Behave! This is a special day for Rio Sagrado, a holy day. Stop disgracing our families!"

Abran squirmed and tugged at his collar while Clemente covered his mouth with his right hand and cleared his throat before speaking, "By the way, where is your Uncle Moisés, Abran?"

"At the store. The railroad people are coming in for supplies."

"*Don* Moisés doesn't seem very religious. Why is that?" queried Isabella.

"Isa, my uncle is a difficult man to explain. I think he -"

The arrival of the Archbishop interrupted Abran. Isabella turned and impulsively reached out to touch the Archbishop's ceremonial staff. Enchanted by her beauty, Lamy stopped and extended his right hand to bless her on her forehead with his thumb. Everyone around her, including Abran and Clemente, somberly crossed themselves while they gazed at a beaming Isabella.

As the two clerics made their way up a short set of stone steps, many of the attendees took a moment to admire the new church. A bell tower topped by a blue wooden cross rose above the brilliant white plaster that covered the adobe bricks. The exposed *vigas* and window frames revealed newly-hewn lumber; a short stone wall that bordered the entire structure provided a striking touch.

Perched atop the front steps of the church, the Archbishop and priest surveyed the crowd as it pressed forward in anticipation. The Archbishop stepped forward and extended a loud, dramatic blessing, *"In nominee Patri, et Filii, et Espiritu Santu...Amen."*

The villagers crossed themselves and repeated in unison, *"Amen."*

Lamy's voice intensified, "We have gathered today to consecrate your new church and rectory. I would like to recognize *Don* Pablo and *Doña* Maria Espinosa for providing the leadership and building materials."

Polite applause greeted *Don* Pablo and *Doña* Maria as they proudly stepped from the front of the clearing and proceeded up the first two steps.

"Don Tomás Lucero and his wife, *Doña* Nicolasa, donated their wonderful carpentry and sewing skills."

The Luceros joined their lifelong friends, the Espinosas, on the steps.

"Don Miguel Valencia served as foreman for this project, while his wife, *Doña* Emilia, supervised the feeding of the workers and volunteers."

The Archbishop waited until all three couples stood together, "The village of Rio Sagrado has proved its worthiness to the Archdiocese of Santa Fe. You have insured the strength of your Catholic faith for years to come. I wish to further congratulate the Espinosa and Lucero families. Their two eldest children, Abran and Isabella, will be the first couple to receive the sacrament of marriage in your new church."

The Archbishop beckoned the young couple forward. Abran and Isabella nervously stepped forward toward the steps. Isabella curtsied in the direction of the Archbishop. Abran appeared more uncomfortable with the unexpected attention than his fiancé. After they received some brief applause from the attendees, the young adults repositioned themselves to face Lamy.

"I have chosen Father Pierre LaSalle to serve as your pastor."

The new priest stepped forward on cue and was greeted by tentative applause. He spoke in a dispassionate tone, "I have come to this village with the purpose of saving your souls. Your duty is to support my efforts in every way. I assume that many of you have not seen a priest in a long time. For this reason, you must attend confession at once."

Abran noticed that some of the people started to grow restless. The priest assumed his previous station and turned toward the Archbishop who now pointed toward the entrance, "Let us proceed inside for the consecration ceremony."

The crowd received one more blessing before they filed in behind Lamy and the benefactors.

Chapter Two

As he approached a partially-constructed adobe house on horseback, Abran surveyed the commotion ahead with some amusement and spurred his mount forward. *Don* Miguel was busy berating four male workers while Clemente pointed to some adobe bricks and lumber that was stacked in front of the house. Abran surprised his uncle and cousin when he galloped up on his horse and dismounted with a flare.

"What brings you here this fine morning?" asked *Don* Miguel.

"*Buenos dias.* I'm on my way to help my uncle move my grandfather's belongings. Why are you shouting at the men?"

"They forgot to cover the adobes and lumber with the tarp last night. Thank God it didn't rain. These *burros* aren't too bright."

"Just don't chase them away, *por favor.* How is my house coming along?"

Clemente answered, "We should be done in a few weeks, if we don't have any more *fiestas.*"

The three men shared a laugh as *Don* Miguel grasped hold of his head, "*Aye,* some of us are still recovering."

"The Archbishop seemed to enjoy the festivities, but I wonder about our new priest," observed Abran.

Clemente rolled his eyes, "I don't think he cared much for our food or wine. Did you see his face when he tasted your father's wine, *primo*?"

"You would have thought he was drinking vinegar."

Don Miguel admonished the duo, "*Silencio!* It's a sin to gossip this way about a priest. Father LaSalle must be used to different things."

A thoughtful silence passed between the three men before Abran swung into action, "*Bueno*, I had better get going. I don't want to anger *Don* Moisés by being late. *Adios, tío*, Cleme."

"*Adios*, Abran. Give my regards to Moisés."

Clemente patted Abran on the shoulder, "Take care, *primo.*"

Abran mounted his horse and urged it forward for a short distance. He reversed direction and deftly guided his mount over the stack of adobe bricks. The workers paused long enough to whistle their approval. Abran let out a rowdy yell as he dashed toward the main road.

Juan Antonio Espinosa, the patriarch of the Espinosa family, passed away two weeks earlier at the age of sixty-eight after a lingering illness leaving his two eldest sons, Moisés and Pablo, to dispose of his belongings as they saw fit. Juan Antonio's devoted wife of forty-three years preceded him in death six years earlier. The major share of the family empire had fallen under Moisés and Pablo's administration over a decade ago. They provided their parents with a comfortable stipend to live out their remaining years. Rather than use the extra space for storage, the siblings decided to rent out their parent's house to a nephew and his growing family.

Several items had already been loaded onto a freight wagon outside. A frustrated, sweat-soaked *Don* Moisés and Abran struggled with a large trunk as the profanities flowed freely. Suddenly, *Don* Moisés' grip faltered and the trunk noisily tumbled onto the earthen floor. Abran started to right the trunk when some items unexpectedly spilled out.

"What is this? I thought the trunk was empty, *tío.*"

"*Sí*, I emptied it yesterday."

"Where did these things come from?"

Abran inspected the inside more closely and removed various items. He held out a panel of wood that's broken in two, "*Mira*, the bottom of the trunk split open, but there's another part... a secret compartment."

The two men examined the various articles and placed them atop a nearby table. Soon, two leather-bound books, ornate head coverings and prayer shawls, a Kiddush cup, and a small menorah covered the tabletop. *Don* Moisés picked up the largest item, a ledger with a worn cover, and turned the pages, "The writing in here is very old."

Abran noticed the bewildered look on his uncle's face after he reached the last pages, "What's wrong?"

"There is an entry here written by my father."

"What does it say?"

September 10, 1830. My name is Juan Antonio Espinosa, the eldest child of Baltasar and Luisa Espinosa. My parents raised their six children both in the Catholic and Jewish faiths. Like my ancestors, we were given Catholic names to hide this practice.

My father passed this book and these other belongings on to me. Our family history is recorded in this book, a proud legacy dating back over three hundred years to Spain, our mother country.

I have decided to raise my children only as Catholics. They do not deserve to be subjected to the dangers of being exposed. I choose to hide their true faith from them. If those who come after me should find these, I pray that it will be a time of tolerance and understanding.

A distressed *Don* Moisés handed the journal to Abran, "My father wrote these words two days before I was born."

At the same time, a brief meeting was taking place between *Don* Pablo and Father LaSalle in the church. They shook hands while they stood in front of the altar.

"I see no problem with your son's requested wedding date. You may proceed with your plans, *Señor* Espinosa."

"Thank you, Father."

"The Archbishop has recommended your appointment as *mayordomo* to which I am in agreement. Congratulations."

"I am honored. Thank you."

Without warning, the priest started walking down the center aisle which forced *Don* Pablo to react quickly, "Evidently your family has acquired a great deal of land and wealth in this valley."

"My forefathers were some of the first Spaniards to settle here. My blessings come from their hard work."

As they arrived at the rear of the church, *Don* Pablo detected a condescending tone in the pastor's next statement, "Your position requires a very strong commitment to our faith. You must set the best example possible. Do you understand, *Señor* Espinosa?"

"Yes, Father."

Father LaSalle motioned toward the nearby confessional, "Very well, it's time for you to confess your sins."

Though stunned by the priest's brusqueness and troubled by his officious manner, *Don* Pablo decided to calmly acquiesce rather than protest. He tilted his head ever so slightly, "Yes, Father."

While seated at his dining room table that evening, *Don* Moisés stared at the articles from the trunk which were laid out in front of him. He scrutinized the Kiddush cup and thought about his father's apprehensions, "Surely there had to be more to my father's decision." He ran his fingertips over the worn leather cover before he opened the journal to read the first entry.

Chapter Three

The first Sunday Mass was about to be held in *La Iglesia de San Ysidro*. The church bell's steady ringing summoned the worshippers. The villagers emerged from their homes dressed in their "Sunday Best" and began making their way on foot toward the house of worship. Others were in the process of arriving by horseback, buggy, and wagon. A visible cloud of dust from the steady traffic lingered about six inches off the ground on the main road. Despite their best effort, many of the women could not prevent a fine coating of dust from settling onto the fringes of their dresses.

The church plaza had turned into an impromptu social center as families exchanged greetings or conversed briefly with their neighbors on their way into the church.

Later, Father LaSalle stared down at his flock from the elevated pulpit and delivered his sermon. Some of the larger families occupied whole pews throughout the sanctuary. He held up a hand-carved *bulto* representing their patron saint, San Ysidro, and spoke "I wish to make an important observation. Many of you have hosted me in your homes this past week and have proudly shown me your crude, homemade icons."

The adults and older adolescents listened dutifully to their pastor while the younger children fidgeted or yawned.

"I have also noticed that many children in this village are rather homely compared to the children back in France."

Many adults stirred uncomfortably and exchanged curious glances.

"There is no doubt in my mind that these unrefined statues manifest the common features in your children." The priest turned toward *Don* Pablo, "Perhaps our *mayordomo* can locate a stock of refined, ceramic saints from back east to sell in his store."

Don Pablo lowered his head and stared self-consciously at his hands. Oblivious to his own tactlessness, Father LaSalle descended from the pulpit and commenced the Celebration of the Eucharist.

Following the Mass, an agitated group including the Espinosas, Luceros, and Valencias, met in the church plaza.

"What can we do about this priest?" pondered *Don* Tomás.

Doña Nicolasa joins in, "Why does he treat us so rudely? To insult our children that way is shameful."

"Do we let him get away with this just because he's a priest?" fretted Doña Emilia.

While the group continued their debate, Abran and Isabella moved toward each other along the perimeter. They came to a stop and maintained a reasonable distance. Abran cautiously looked around for a moment, "You are more beautiful than any woman in France."

Isabella tried to conceal her blushing face with an ornate fan, "Stop that! You're going to get us in trouble."

"I don't care. It's worth it just to see you smile." Abran stepped closer and touched her arm lightly, "*Te amo*, Isa. With all my heart."

Overwhelmed by her fiancé's declaration, Isabella struggled with her reply, "*Te... te amo*, Abran."

A hissing sound diverted their attention to Clemente, who proceeded to tap on his ear. He motioned toward the small gathering. Abran and Isabelle casually approached him. "The *viejitos* are on the warpath," whispered Clemente. The curious trio observed their elders' deliberations.

"Pablo, you're the *mayordomo*. Go talk to the *padre* for us," pleaded *Don* Miguel.

Doña Maria challenged this tactic, "What can he do, Miguel? A priest's authority cannot be questioned."

"I'm talking about his respect, not his authority. Talk to him man-to-man."

Everyone awaited *Don* Pablo's reply, "Our priest is a headstrong man. I don't think he would listen very well."

Doña Maria made another observation that seemed to calm down her companions, "What would happen if the priest removes Pablo for speaking up? Who would be the new *mayordomo*?"

Don Tomás directed his gaze toward Father LaSalle, who was being approached by Samuel Ortiz, an inelegant man who moved with a stooped, self-conscious gait, "Maybe he'd make Samuel Ortiz the new *mayordomo. Mira ese desgrac...*"

Doña Nicolasa quickly covered her husband's mouth with her hand before he completed his insult, "Don't say that word, especially on a Sunday!"

The assemblage watched as the priest and Samuel shook hands. As they walked toward the rectory, *Don* Pablo prophetically voiced his misgivings, "This can't be good."

Father LaSalle and Samuel Ortiz sat across from each other in the kitchen; Samuel spoke first, "As I told you the other day, I would like to offer my services to you."

"What do you have in mind?"

"Well it seems that the Espinosas and their cronies have seized control of everything in the valley. Even this church."

"Let me remind you that I'm the one in control here, Señor Ortiz."

"Forgive me, Father."

Initially the priest found the parishioner's homely features and rumpled appearance distasteful. Reluctantly, he agreed to this meeting. Now the priest sensed an advantage and decided to continue, "You seem to hold a grudge against the Espinosas."

"Their father used his mercantile store to swindle my father out of most of our land. *Don* Pablo and *Don* Moisés are no better."

"*Don* Moisés? Who is he?"

"*Don* Pablo's older brother."

"This is the first I have heard of him."

"He's a mean-spirited man. Not very religious either."

Father LaSalle drew his clasped hands to his chin and deliberated for a moment. The bitterness in Samuel's voice along with his revelations prompted the priest to carefully consider his next response. He sensed that, despite Samuel's dubious nature, the miscreant might serve an informative purpose.

"Perhaps I need to be wary of this Moisés fellow. Do you agree Señor Ortiz?"

"Oh yes, Father."

"I require someone to be on the lookout for any unusual behavior that a parish priest should know about."

The priest fixed his gaze upon Samuel. It took a few seconds for Samuel to grasp LaSalle's intent, "Of course, *padre*."

"In the meantime, I think I should introduce myself to this Moisés."

Father LaSalle hastily dismissed Samuel Ortiz and reflected upon the significance of this new information.

Like many *haciendas* of the period, a large patio occupied the interior space of *Don* Pablo's residence. In earlier times, cattle were herded into the spacious opening from nearby pastures and corrals when marauding Comanches and their allies invaded the valley. The adobe walls, along with thick window shutters and heavy wooden doors, protected the inhabitants and domestic animals. During more peaceful times, many of the household chores occurred here, as well as important family functions.

Many of the extended members of the Espinosa and Lucero families were gathered for a Sunday meal. The adults and older children, including Abran and Isabella, were seated at larger tables, while the younger children occupied smaller tables nearby. *Don* Tomás stood after he filled his goblet with wine and proposed a toast, "To our gracious hosts and future in-laws, *Los Espinosas.*"

The other attendees responded, "*¡Salud!*"

Everyone drank from their goblet. *Don* Pablo stood and raised his goblet, "To the blessed union of Isabella and Abran."

"*¡Salud!*"

Doñas Nicolasa and Maria rose from their seats on cue. They giggled while reciting their toast in unison. "May they bless us with many precious grandchildren."

"*¡Salud!*"

Abran started refilling the adults' goblets with wine while Isabella replenished the younger children's goblets from a pitcher. They returned to their stations; Isabella proposed her own toast, "To our wonderful parents. Your support and love mean everything to us."

Abran interjected, "Especially when we'll need their help changing the diapers of our nine or ten children."

Many of the family members broke into laughter. "*¡Salud!*"

Don Pablo and *Doña* Maria walked over to a covered item and pulled a canvas sheet off an elegant trunk. *Don* Pablo motioned for Isabella to join them, "Isabella, it is my honor to present you with your trousseau. We hope that you will find it satisfactory."

Isabella clumsily hugged *Don* Pablo as he tried to hand her the keys, *Doña* Maria also received a vigorous hug. "*Gracias, Don* Pablo, *Doña* Maria."

"Congratulations, *hija.* Remember that we women cherish our trunks more than our husbands." Laughter breaks out from several of the family members.

Curious family members flocked to the trunk and observed Isabella as she unlocked it. She removed a beautiful wedding dress and veil, which elicited collective comments of admiration. In the meantime, the adult males wisely made their getaway into the house, where they drank whiskey and swapped their latest tales of bravado.

Chapter Four

The Espinosa Mercantile Store had sat in its present location for over forty years and had undergone numerous expansions. The original adobe edifice eventually merged with newer wooden-exterior additions. The advent of the Santa Fe Trail in the 1820's provided an unforeseen boon to the family fortunes. After crossing the Rio Sagrado at the village of San Miguel del Vado, the American traders had but a short journey to Santa Fe. Unfortunately, their route bypassed Rio Sagrado by about six miles. Initially, pack mules were the chief conveyers of trade goods, but these soon yielded to covered wagons due to the high demand for the *americano* goods and the wagons' greater carrying capacity.

Baltasar Espinosa possessed the foresight to coax the early traders to venture into nearby Rio Sagrado before proceeding on to Santa Fe. This monopoly lasted for several years until Baltasar decided to purchase a pair of covered wagons and joined other *Nuevo Mexicanos* in forming their own wagon trains to Missouri. Juan Antonio, starting at the young age of twelve, accompanied his father and uncles on their demanding journeys to Independence, Missouri.

As teenagers, Moisés and Pablo joined their father and acquired valuable knowledge that allowed them to discern their neighbors' needs and transact business with their American suppliers. Younger siblings eventually took over the trading excursions or managed the smaller stores in the outlying communities like La Cueva and Cañoncito while Moisés and Pablo concentrated their energies on the overall operations. In addition to trading goods and supplies, the Espinosas decided to invest in the equipment that enabled them to build a sawmill that broadened the family's commercial interests.

On this particular day, *Don* Moisés was leaning over a counter while recording some transactions onto a ledger. He was too engrossed in the undertaking to notice the approaching stranger.

"Are you Moisés Espinosa?" queried Father LaSalle.

Don Moisés looked up and responded with a nod. The priest offered a handshake, but *Don* Moisés chose to ignore the gesture and retained his grip on the quill pen in his right hand. "I am Pierre LaSalle, your new parish priest."

"Ah, the French priest who considers our children ugly."

Father LaSalle withdrew his handshake and crossed his arms, "Why haven't I seen you in church?"

"Because, I haven't been there."

"But weren't you born into the Faith? It is your duty to serve the Church."

Don Moisés laid the pen down and straightened his posture, "My duty is to maintain our family enterprises with my brother."

"How can you ignore the Faith that you were baptized into?"

"Because your God stole two loving wives from me before they could bear any children."

"Don't you fear eternal damnation?"

"I wonder about the many superstitions that your Faith spreads. Maybe there is no such thing as eternal damnation."

The pastor clutched the crucifix hanging around his neck. This verbal jousting reminded him of his childhood days in France before he was sent to the seminary, and of the competitive fencing bouts with his older brother who was anointed successor to the family's aristocratic fortunes. He assumed that his superior intellect and ecclesiastical training would easily overcome this simple peasant's assertions.

"Cease you blasphemy, *Señor* Espinosa."

Don Moisés sensed his advantage, "I have only provided answers to your questions." He found it amusing when the priest directed the Sign of the Cross at him while mumbling a prayer. *Don* Moisés couldn't resist the urge to fire one more volley, "I am curious to know what order you belong to?"

"The Franciscan Order. Why do you ask?"

"Ah, the Franciscans. I've read about their role as henchman for the Vatican."

The priest's face flushed with anger, "Impossible. Where did you read these lies?"

"Of course, the Franciscans' infamy pales in comparison to the Dominicans' doesn't it?"

"What do you mean?"

"I speak of the campaign waged against the French and Spanish Jews by your order and *los Domino-canos.*"

"Your reference to my Dominican brothers insults my God."

"*Domino Canos.* Isn't that Latin for God's dogs? Only animals would contrive an injustice like the Inquisition."

"Enough. You speak of events long past."

"But not forgotten."

Father LaSalle realized that he had lost considerable ground in this battle of wits and tried to salvage his dignity, "So where did you read about these lies?"

"A history book, I think."

"Perhaps you could show me this book sometime."

"Perhaps not. I don't remember what became of it."

"You tread on dangerous ground, *señor*. You must take your salvation more seriously."

"And if I don't?"

"Grave consequences could result."

"I will take my chances then. Your authority means nothing in this store."

Don Moisés derived a perverse pleasure in watching as Father LaSalle pivoted around and exited through the front entrance. Dealing with dishonest *americanos* in Missouri or corrupt *politicos* in Santa Fe had honed his cleverness over the past decades. This pretentious cleric presented no threat to *Don* Moisés' pending objective.

Chapter Five

The stunning New Mexico sunset cast an unearthly glow upon the west-facing walls of *Don* Moisés' adobe house. Inside, a setting of elegant blue-white china and distinctly-patterned silverware for two people, was spread atop the dining table. A bottle of wine sat next to a long loaf of bread. Several candles remained unlit.

Don Moisés and Abran stood next to a large desk that dominated the adjoining room that serves as *Don* Moisés' study. The items from the trunk were laid out for Abran to view. *Don* Moisés swept his right hand over the collection, "I have spent time learning about the articles we found in my father's trunk. Our family history is strongly connected to these things."

"Why do you choose to tell me this, *tío*?"

"You're the closest thing to a son that I have. Please indulge an old man."

"But knowing these things could be dangerous. Isn't that why my grandfather made his decision?"

"Only because of people's ignorance. The Church insures this by spreading lies against the Jews."

"But does it matter to God whether we are Catholic or Jew?"

"The Jews, our people, were God's chosen ones long before this Christian madness began."

"This still seems risky. The villagers are already gossiping about your angering Father LaSalle the other day."

"You let me worry about that priest. Let me tell you about these articles and then join me for dinner. I had my housekeeper cook up a special meal."

"It smells very delicious. What's the occasion?"

"It's called a *Shabbat* and takes place from sundown on Friday to sundown on Saturday."

By the time he stood before the dining table, Abran's head was still spinning from the just-concluded orientation. *Don* Moisés had leafed through the family journal and revealed the many entries encapsulating almost four hundred years of Espinosa family history. Some of them proved difficult to read due to the varying qualities of inks used and styles of penmanship. The other book in the trunk was a Jewish Bible written in Spanish, which amazed Abran. *Don* Moisés explained the significance of the menorah, the prayer shawl and the yarmulke. Before he entered the dining room, *Don* Moisés had wrapped the prayer shawl around his shoulders and placed the yarmulke atop his head. An uneasy Abran declined his uncle's invitation to do the same.

Don Moisés removed a cover from a platter exposing a garnished roast. He struggled briefly with the prayer shawl while lighting the candles, "One of the writings in the journal states that the candle's glow means that God sends us an extra soul on *Shabbat*."

He bowed his head after unfolding a piece of paper, "Our God and the God of ages past, may our rest be acceptable to You; hallow us by Your commandments; satisfy us with Your goodness; gladden us with Your salvation; and purify our hearts to serve You in truth."

Don Moisés passed the Kiddush cup to Abran; he handed it back after drinking a small amount of wine. *Don* Moisés then took a drink, set the cup down and motioned for Abran to seat himself. The *Shabbat* feast commenced.

Father LaSalle summoned *Don* Pablo to an impromptu Saturday morning meeting. Normally they wouldn't see each other until the late afternoon to make the necessary preparations for the coming week. Because Saturday mornings were one of the busiest times for the mercantile store, the meeting proved to be a great inconvenience for *Don* Pablo. Now he found himself seated across from Father LaSalle, at the same table where the priest and Samuel Ortiz had met six days earlier. "Your brother's conduct displeases me, *señor*. What do you intend to do about this?"

"Father, I'm not sure what I can do."

"This is a very serious matter, one that could result in his ex-communication."

"Is that really necessary?"

"He could use his influential position to corrupt others."

Don Pablo felt his stomach growing uneasy. All his brother had done was challenge the authority of this boorish priest. Unfortunately, some of the villagers happened to be in the store and overheard the exchange. The gossip spread quickly. Perhaps the *padre* was more concerned about his damaged ego and chose to cloak it with this ridiculous reprimand. "Corrupt others? My brother can be very outspoken, but I wouldn't consider him a menace to the Church."

"Your son, Abran, appears to be falling under his persuasion."

"What do you mean?"

"There appeared to be some sort of clandestine meeting between them last night."

"It was a simple dinner, Father. Moisés holds Abran in special favor since he has no children of his own."

"Perhaps it was more than a dinner. It's been reported to me that some strange rituals took place, maybe acts of sorcery. I suggest that you look into the matter."

"I will, Father. But the source of your information concerns me, especially since he associates with known thieves and drunkards."

Don Pablo's rebuttal unnerved the priest. He tensely fussed with the sleeves of his frock while trying to remember the other matter he had intended to broach. An awkward moment passed until the priest spoke, "Are you aware of any books in your brother's possession, a history book perhaps?"

"Moisés and I share what few books we own. I don't recall such a book. Why do you ask?"

"No reason in particular. History is one of my favorite subjects. Good books are hard to find out here."

Don Pablo stood and stared anxiously at the door, "With your indulgence, I need to get back to the store. It's proving to be a very busy day."

Father LaSalle waved as if he was more annoyed than placated, "Yes, by all means go. But remember what we discussed today. I'll expect immediate results, *señor.*"

"Yes, Father. *Buenos Dias.*"

An encounter later that evening between the two brothers in *Don* Pablo's patio evolved into an unpleasant affair. In anticipation, Abran's siblings had been herded into an isolated room within the *hacienda* to safeguard the sensitive matter at hand. *Doña* Maria and Abran were the only witnesses to *Don* Pablo and Moisés' unyielding argument. Finally, an exasperated *Don* Pablo sat down after throwing both his arms in the air.

Doña Maria rose from her chair, "You two must quit acting like *burros.* Moisés, you went too far when you antagonized the priest."

"He has no authority over me, Maria."

"Pablo and I put a lot of work into our new church."

"But our past is different. Our real faith - "

"Enough with that! Our father made a wise choice, the only choice that made sense," protested *Don* Pablo.

Doña Maria cautioned her brother-in-law, "Moisés, you need to be more careful with your words and actions. Leave the past alone!"

Abran interrupted the brief contemplation that ensued, "*Tío*, please excuse. I don't understand many of the things you've shown me. They seem important to you, but my wedding means everything to me. And to Isabella."

Doña Maria noticed *Don* Moisés impatience, "Listen carefully to your *sobrino*. You're always bragging to others about how sensible and smart he is."

"All we ask is that you think of who will pay the consequences for your actions. *Por favor, hermano,*" beseeched *Don* Pablo.

All eyes were upon *Don* Moisés who mulled over the dilemma. "Very well, then. I'll try my best to stay out of the priest's way."

The two brothers reconciled while *Doña* Maria proudly kissed Abran's cheek.

Chapter Six

Ever since he could recall, Moisés Espinosa never felt a true connection to the Catholic Faith that his parents espoused. Even the local *Penitentes*, a brotherhood of male villagers devoted to maintaining the Catholic faith and performing penance, especially during Holy Week, or the itinerant Mexican priests who ventured from Santa Fe to Rio Sagrado to perform weddings and baptisms, failed to capture his interest or arouse his soul. Nor did the faith practiced in his domicile by his two young wives. Losing his first wife, Elena, in childbirth and his second, Rachel, to influenza had diminished his belief in a just God and fostered a deep resentment within Moisés.

The discovery of the trunk's contents and the recorded accounts of the Espinosa family transformed Moisés in ways he never expected. It took forty-nine years of living to find the missing element that gave his life meaning beyond the family enterprises. Claiming his Jewish birthright had become *Don* Moisés' chief passion despite the presence of the intrusive priest. Abran's reluctance to participate in this righteous quest was his one regret.

Alone in his house this Friday evening, *Don* Moisés was reciting the *Shabbat* prayer as the candle flames flickered around the table. He started to sit down to dinner after drinking from the Kiddush cup. Suddenly, he heard a commotion outside and shouted out "Who's there?"

A familiar voice answered. "It's me, Abran. Come see what I've caught."

Don Moisés stepped out onto the back porch. The twilight revealed a figure lying on the ground. Abran's right boot pressed down on the intruder as he pulled tautly on a rope. "Who's this?"

"Our old friend. He tried to run away, but my rope was too quick for him."

Don Moisés stooped down for a closer look. Decades of loathing welled up within him when he recognized the captive, Samuel Ortiz. The bad blood between the Espinosa and Ortiz families had spanned several generations simply because the Ortiz ancestors tended to covet the Espinosa's hard-earned possessions. In fact, it had become a family tradition to warn impressionable Espinosa offspring at an early age about the deceitful, larcenous proclivities of the Ortiz *malcriados*. "What are you doing here, *cabrón*?"

"Let go of me! I saw a wild animal and came to alert you."

"Liar. I caught sight of him sneaking down here to spy on you," reports Abran.

"That's not true, you - "

Don Moisés delivered a swift kick to Samuel's ribs which resulted in an unsettling groan. "Be careful with your words, you're on my property."

Samuel struggled for breath, "Yes, forgive me. Now will you let me go?"

"Why? So you can go and speak your lies to that priest?"

"This is all a misunderstanding. I meant no harm."

Abran pressed down harder with his boot. *Don* Moisés deliberately waited a few seconds before he signaled Abran to release the squirming trespasser. Abran roughly pulled Samuel to his feet and loosened the rope. Suddenly, Samuel bolted into the darkness and tripped over some unseen obstacle. "Goddamn it!"

Don Moisés and Abran laughed loudly; *Don* Moisés shouted out, "You better get your filthy mouth to confession."

Don Moisés turned to Abran. "Come inside and join me for dinner."

Abran gazed nervously toward his parent's house. "*Gracias, tío*, but I had better get back."

The two exchanged a brief hug before going their separate ways. "*Bueno*, thanks for your help, Abran."

Abran was conversing with Isabella and her parents prior to attending Sunday Mass when something out of the corner of his eye diverted his attention. Samuel Ortiz limped toward them; scratches were visible on his face. Abran's posture suddenly changed from a relaxed, upright one to a hostile stance with both fists clenched. Samuel quickly veered away when he realized where he was headed. Isabella exchanged a quizzical glance with her parents.

Later, Father LaSalle was in the process of concluding his lengthy homily to the congregation. "Before we proceed with the Celebration of the Eucharist, I must warn you of certain evil influences present in this village."

Many heads turned toward each other as they whispered comments of speculation and anxiety. Abran noticed a fleeting smile on the priest's face during the commotion. A raised left hand hushed the crowd. "Beware of any unusual behavior, especially at night."

The wooden floor creaked in response to the numerous startled bodies as Father LaSalle's fist slammed against the oak lectern. "But be assured that these heretics will be severely punished by the Church!"

As the villagers sat in stunned silence, Abran noticed the agonized look on his father's face.

The time to receive Communion finally arrived and the congregation made their way to the Communion rail that separated the altar from the worshippers. The first wave knelt while waiting for Father LaSalle to dispense the Eucharist. An altar boy held a brass dish under each recipient's chin. Upon reaching Abran, the priest nudged the acolyte's hand to the next person. Abran maintained his position until the last person had been served.

He stood to address Father LaSalle who had headed back toward the altar. "Why didn't you serve me Communion?"

The assembly registered its collective shock as the priest abruptly turned around to face Abran. "How dare you interrupt this Mass! You are unworthy of this sacrament."

The stunned altar boy didn't know what to do when the chalice was handed to him. His eyes pleaded for guidance from someone, anyone. Upon reaching Abran, the enraged priest paused for a moment and then slapped the young man on the cheek. "You must cleanse your soul of your uncle's evil. I will not allow you back into this church until you repent."

The parishioners' agitation escalated. Abran touched his left cheek as tears trickled down both sides. "But I have done nothing wrong, Father."

He rushed down the main aisle toward the rear entrance. Many congregants turned their heads to follow Abran's exit. Isabella impulsively ran after her fiancé, followed closely by Clemente.

They stood near the spot where they had earlier exchanged pleasantries. A distraught Isabella clung to Abran while Clemente's right hand rested on his cousin's right shoulder before he expressed his concerns, "That priest had no right to do that. Someone must be filling his head with lies."

Isabella wondered aloud, "But who would deceive Father LaSalle, Cleme?"

Clemente exchanged a knowing glance with his cousin. "I warned you, Abran. He's getting even for Friday night."

The front door to the church suddenly opened. Abran and Isabella's parents hurried down the steps which obliged the couple to separate. *Doña* Maria was the first to speak, followed by *Doña* Nicolasa. "*Hijos, hija,* come back into the church. We'll straighten this out with the *padre* after Mass."

"*Sí,* your fathers will fix everything."

Abran was quick to protest, "Stop it! Can't you see what's really going on?"

"Abran, don't," cautioned Isabella.

"The only evil around here is that *pinche* priest and that *lámbe* Samuel Ortiz."

Doña Maria gasped as she drew a hand to her mouth, "*¡Válgame Dios!*"

Don Pablo interjected, "*Hijo,* your words will only make things worse."

"You all are so afraid of the priest. You won't even defend my innocence."

"That's not true. We just have to be careful."

"All that you care about is that I've embarrassed both of you. Maybe I should leave so I won't shame you anymore."

A fretful *Doña* Maria stepped toward her son but was restrained by *Don* Pablo. Abran issued a parting edict, "Go inside and do whatever your priest tells you!"

Abran started walking away, but paused when Isabella runs up to him. "Abran, our wedding. What can we do?"

"*¿Quién sabe,* Isa?"

"Abran."

Abran kissed Isabella on the forehead and brushed the tears off her cheek, "I'm sorry, but no one can treat me this way."

Isabella watched helplessly as Abran strode briskly toward his horse. Without warning, Clemente sprinted over to join his cousin, "Wait up, *primo.*"

Abran delayed his departure until they could gallop off together toward his home where he gathered some essential belongings with Clemente's assistance. Arriving at *Don* Moisés' house, a distraught Abran recounted the earlier events and asked his uncle's permission to move in with him. Initially, *Don* Moisés was reluctant to agree since he wished to avoid aggravating his brother. Abran refused to return, given the lack of support from his parents. He reminded his uncle that this predicament resulted because of the *Shabbat* and Samuel Ortiz's revenge. Clemente urged *Don* Moisés to consider approaching Abran's parents to convince them that Abran's stay would be a temporary arrangement and could serve as a cooling off period between everyone concerned. *Don* Moisés pondered the proposal and decided to champion this cause. He invited Abran to move into a spare bedroom.

After he settled in, Abran began to read the family journal at the behest of his uncle and discovered a centuries-old legacy of secrecy and exile.

Chapter Seven

Spain's most momentous year, 1492, was also her most regrettable for centuries to come. After defeating the last remaining Moorish stronghold near Granada, King Ferdinand of Aragon and Queen Isabella of Castile were able to unite Spain under one rule and guide her destiny into a new era. Supporting Christoforo Columbo's bold venture would usher in the legendary *El Siglo de Oro*, The Century of Gold, which enabled Spain to acquire unimagined riches from the Americas, gold, silver, and proprietary plant life.

Ignoring the tripartite economy, comprised of Christians, Jewish, and Moorish citizens that had flourished under the Umayyad and Almohade's rule for over eight hundred years, Ferdinand and Isabella foolishly issued The Edict of Expulsion in late March declaring that the only Jews permitted to remain in Spain were those who wished to convert. Two days prior to Colombo's August 3rd departure from the port of Palos (near Huelva) in southern Spain, the departure deadline for unconverted Jews drove away some of Spain's most talented citizens while forcing the remaining *conversos* into a life of constant fear and secrecy.

The lack of an adequate medical, financial, and administrative infrastructure exacted a toll on Spain's fortunes over time. Spain's riches and opulent spending would eventually empower her capitalistic Protestant neighbors. Ironically, Spain's Jewish population totaled only a half million out of seven million; but one year after the Edict of Expulsion, rents in Sevilla dropped by one-half of what they had been.

The Guadalquivir River made it possible for Sevilla to serve as the maritime capital of the Spanish Empire. Designated as the royal port, Sevilla would become the most important trade center for Spain as goods and precious metals flowed in from the New World. Finally, the creation of the Casa de Contratacion would control Spain's colonial commerce fostering Sevilla's financial and cultural prosperity that would cultivate the talents of noted artists like Francisco de Zurbarán, Diego Velázquez, and Bartolome Esteban Murillo.

The well-appointed house and adjacent warehouses embodied the commercial acumen of *Don* Solomon de Espinosa. His reputation as a purveyor of quality, imported goods was exceeded only by his prominence in the province's social and political structure. A balcony offered a vantage point for a distressed *Don* Solomon who took a respite from his first journal entry. He stared down at the street below crowded with overloaded wagons and handcarts. The traffic flowed in the direction of the Guadalquivir harbor where several ships were anchored nearby.

"I am witness to a great tragedy this day, August 1, 1492. By Royal Decree, my Jewish brothers and sisters have been banished from our homeland. Our proud presence endured over 1,500 years in Spain. Through the ages, our fathers contributed to a great legacy. Rabbi Moses ben Nahman was a great Biblical Scholar and Talmudic Scholar. Moses ben Maimon (Maimonides) enlightened our world with his wisdom and knowledge."

Don Solomon witnessed a desperate scene as he peered through a spyglass. Persons of all ages struggled up the gangplank of a Spanish ship with their belongings while various articles float in the water. An officer ordered a trunk to be thrown overboard. A woman protested, while her husband pleaded with the officer. Some gold coins were handed over allowing the trunk to be placed into the ship's hold.

The navigational charts and maps that empowered this country were created by Jewish minds. The same is true for the quadrant that helps determine a vessel's position at sea. Our Muslim and Catholic Rulers prospered because of notable Jewish men who managed their affairs. Two of our leaders, Don Isaac Abrabenel and Abraham Seneor, fought to have the Expulsion Decree revoked. It is said that King Ferdinand accepted a large bribe, but ignored their pleas.

Solomon de Espinosa returned to his desk to resume his writing.

I choose to remain here veiled in a cloak of secrecy. I refuse to forfeit my wealth to the greedy dogs that profit from this misery. I draw my inspiration from the great Maimonides and will continue my deception. The barbaric Inquisition casts its ugly shadow over this once noble country. I risk much with this journal's first entry, but hope that it will enlighten my descendants in the uncertain future. Solomon de Espinosa.

Fortune favored *Don* Solomon and his progeny in the centuries to come. *Don* Solomon never imagined that his journal would survive beyond a few generations when he recorded the first of several observations. Most of all, he dreaded its discovery by the religious or civil authorities who might persecute his heirs because of its contents. But every succeeding generation produced a male heir who safeguarded the legacy and concocted ingenious ways to conceal the journal as it made its unexpected journey to New Spain and the isolated frontier to the north.

Archbishop Lamy perused a document while seated behind a large desk opposite Father LaSalle. A leather bag full of coins sat to the side. "I am pleased with your progress so far, Pierre. The financial support of your new parish is impressive."

"Thank you, *Seigneurie.*"

"Are you prepared for Father Bernard's visit?'

"*Oui.* Bernard and I have a lot of catching up to do."

"I thought you could help prepare him for his new assignment."

"I thank you for your confidence."

"Are there any other matters that I need to consider?"

Father LaSalle hesitated for a moment, "There is one other matter, a rather grave one."

The Archbishop granted his cautious consent, "Go on."

"It concerns the excommunication of a baptized villager. I have received reports of suspicious activities. He even refuses to attend Mass."

Lamy leaned forward with a stern look on his face, "Pierre, excommunication is a serious matter. It must not be arbitrary or vindictive in nature. Have you attempted to reason with this person?"

"I tried to engage him in conversation, but found him to be antagonistic toward the Church."

"This is most unusual. If we consider excommunication, do you think it would return this person to the path of righteousness?"

"I hope so, *Seigneurie.* He has already influenced a young member of my flock and could influence others as well."

The priest discerned his superior's more grave tone, "We must make sure that this action achieves the intended result, *prêtre.* After all, this is a new parish. Your flock must view this as medicinal in nature, not punitive."

Father LaSalle retrieved some folded papers from his valise and handed them over to the Archbishop, "I have documented the evidence thoroughly. There's one other thing I should disclose to you."

Lamy diverted his gaze from the report. "The villager in question is Moisés Espinosa, brother of Pablo. The young man I alluded to is Pablo's son, Abran."

"Blessed Saint Francis! This is going to be more difficult than I thought."

The priest watched as Lamy retrieved a pen and a piece of paper from a desk drawer. Without delay, the Archbishop drafted a letter and sealed it with candle wax and a signet; he handed the communiqué to Father LaSalle. "Share this with *Don* Pablo upon your return tomorrow. I have found him to be a very reasonable man. Work this matter out with him, Pierre."

"I will."

Father LaSalle excused himself from the Archbishop's presence.

Alone at last, Jean Baptiste Lamy suddenly felt the effects of his many decades of duty and diligence as he pondered the prospect of another ex-communication. Numerous battles were fought following his arrival in August, 1851, accompanied by his aide, Joseph Machebeuf. The ecclesiastical transition from the Mexican Diocese of Durango under Bishop José Antonio Zubiría y Escalante to the New Mexico Vicariate (which would be elevated to the Diocese of Santa Fe in late 1853) led by a Frenchman divided the loyalties of several resident clergy. As one would expect, culture clashes and power struggles exacted their toll.

The alienation of two notable priests, Padre Antonio José Martinez of Taos and Padre José Manuel Gallegos of Albuquerque, over a short period of time generated its share of controversy. The machinations of Vicar Machebeuf in these matters and numerous others, some of them occurring during Lamy's absences while on church business to Baltimore and Europe, caused many bitter feelings. Accusations that Machebeuf had violated the seal of confession by revealing certain information during sermons in various parishes beleaguered Archbishop Lamy until the powers in Rome cleared his aide of the charges in 1856. Four years later, Machebeuf was sent to Colorado to tend to the territory's burgeoning population, fueled by the discovery of gold and silver deposits. He later served as Denver's first Bishop starting in 1868.

Archbishop Lamy was now forced to contend with the presence of the Protestant churches, the Methodists and Presbyterians in particular, who stole Catholic souls every day and weakened the Church's foundation in the nearby communities.

He prayed for the Holy Spirit to guide Father LaSalle since the last thing the Archdiocese needed was a public dispute that would reflect badly on the Church.

Isabella stood next to Clemente while several children frolicked in a small clearing next to the Rio Sagrado. She looked over her shoulder in the direction of some nearby cottonwood trees. Clemente exhorted her to take action, "Go on, he's waiting for you."

"Are you sure that I should do this?"

"Don't worry about the children, I'll keep them distracted."

"This is a bad time for anyone to see us together, Clemente. Father LaSalle might find out."

Clemente nudged Isabella on her way, "*¡Andalé!* This isn't the first time we've done this."

After she took a few steps, Isabella turned back to face Clemente who motioned her forward. Isabella found Abran hiding behind a large tree; they embraced while kissing passionately.

Abran stroked Isabella's face tenderly, "I missed you so much, Isa."

"And I missed you."

They kissed again and peered through an opening in the trees. Abran wrapped his hands around Isabella's waist as they watched Clemente playing with Isabella's siblings. Countless shouts and screams of contentment filled the air. Clemente directed some special attention to Agapita, Isabella's winsome sixteen year-old sister, "My cousin comes through for us again."

"You are lucky to have such a trusted *compañero*. But I also think he helps out so he can flirt with Agapita."

Abran gently turned Isabella around and rested his forehead against hers. "Will the picnics with our children be just as noisy?"

"I hope so, Abran. Lots of noise from lots of children, *¿qué no?*"

They moved over to a nearby log and sat down.

"I can hardly wait for that day."

"But how will we ever marry? You have offended our priest."

Abran's voice rose in anger, "He had no right to treat me that way."

Isabella placed her hand on his knee, "I know, but your actions since then haven't helped matters."

"What does it matter? Being accused is the same as being guilty."

"Not everyone feels that way, especially those who love you."

"That *entremetido* is mistaken about my uncle. He isn't a *brujo*. He, we have discovered some things about our family's history, important things."

"What are they?"

Abran directed his gaze to a distant spot, "I can't tell you now, someday soon perhaps."

Without warning, Abran grabbed Isabella's hands, "Isa, let's just run off and get married in Santa Fe by one of those magistrates."

"Oh no, Abran. That would be disgraceful. Our children would be illegitimate in the eyes of the Church."

A despondent Abran stared away for several seconds before he faced his intended, "Just be patient. I'll try to find a solution so we can be together."

Isabella reached out to touch his cheek, "I'll pray every day to our Blessed Mother. A lot of people are praying for us."

A distant whistle interrupted their interlude. Abran helped Isabella to her feet. They embraced and kissed one final time. "You better get back, Isa."

He wiped the tears from her face with his fingertips and guided her to the edge of the tree line. Abran sadly watched as Isabella returned to her rowdy siblings and Clemente.

Chapter Eight

*D*on Pablo *and Doña* Maria met once again with *Don* Moisés in the patio of *Don* Pablo's *hacienda.* *Don* Pablo handed the Archbishop's letter to his brother, "I wanted to give you this before we discuss the railroad contract. It's from the Archbishop."

"Why does he bother writing me?"

"He's concerned about your confrontation with Father LaSalle. You could be excommunicated from the Church."

"Why should my behavior concern the Archbishop?"

"*Hermano*, this is a very grave matter."

"You've even dragged Abran into this mess," added *Doña* Maria.

Don Moisés nonchalantly held up the dispatch, "I'll read what he has to say, but his threat means nothing to me."

Don Pablo pounded his fist against the table which startled his wife and brother, "Damn it, Moisés! This affair affects everybody, not just you and that arrogant priest."

Doña Maria offered a more serious perspective, "Our position in this village could be damaged forever."

Don Pablo placed his left arm around his wife's shoulders, "Please don't act impulsively. Father LaSalle expects an answer by the end of the week."

"I'll carefully consider my response, Pablo. Now, can we discuss the railroad contract?"

Don Pablo looked over to *Doña* Maria and shrugged his shoulder. His brother continued, "I wanted to take Abran with me to Kansas City after I sign the contract. He needs to learn all that he can about our enterprises."

"That's fine with me. What do you think Maria?"

"It would be good for him to become more familiar with the *americano* ways."

Don Moisés casually tossed the letter aside and opened a business ledger, "Here's what I've calculated. I'll share this with Abran later."

The Atchison, Topeka, and Santa Fe Railroad basically followed the same route as the Santa Fe Trail. New towns with American names sprang up along the steel rails that traversed the northeastern New Mexico grasslands. Accessible markets for once remote ranching and farming hamlets now presented the pioneers with new commercial prospects. Upon reaching Las Vegas, the railroad created an unexpected partition when it bypassed the old town plaza and laid its track on the other side of the Gallinas River. This partition resulted in the founding of a predominantly *gringo* East Las Vegas, while the original, predominantly Hispanic town became known as West Las Vegas.

The next phase running from Las Vegas to Albuquerque produced new opportunities for the Espinosa family. Raw timber and an idle workforce were plentiful in the Upper Rio Sagrado valley; the Rio Sagrado sawmill could easily handle the extra demand. By virtue of their current contract to supply its survey teams, the Santa Fe Railroad was already familiar with Espinosas' efficiency and accepted their proposal to supply the needed railroad ties and timber.

An energetic Father LaSalle hoped to impress his old seminary mate, Bernard Pitaval, with a first-rate display of hospitality. His housekeeper, Rosa Flores, had labored to prepare the rectory under the priest's endless scrutiny and tolerated the priest's audacity when he forced his limited culinary expertise upon her during her dinner preparations. The *padre* surprised *Don* Pablo with a request for two bottles of his finest wine, which was graciously granted. When the portly Frenchman finally arrived, *Señora* Flores was thankful that the visitor kept Father LaSalle out of her hair. She prayed that the next five days would be more bearable than the past three.

The two priests helped themselves to the second bottle of wine after dinner. Father LaSalle offered his thanksgiving, "I'm relieved that your journey went well, Bernard. There are so many hazards out here that can waylay even the hardiest of travelers."

"Thank you, Pierre. The Blessed Virgin and Saint Christopher kept a careful watch over me."

The host raised his goblet to offer a toast. "To the Blessed Virgin… "

His guest grinned mischievously while responding. "y *todos los santos*."

After sipping the wine, a disgusted look registered on Father LaSalle's face as he set the goblet down, "I really must apologize for this native wine. Like everything else around here, it is a bit uncouth."

"It's not so bad. I think I could acquire a taste for it."

"You're a brave soul, *paysan*."

"Your new assignment appears to be going well, Pierre. What advice do you have to offer?"

"This is an isolated place, somewhat backwards and uncivilized. You will come to miss the refinements of our mother country."

"But I've seen beauty even in the most barren of landscapes."

"Your opinion will change when you get to know these people. Their isolation has cultivated some crude practices."

"But they are Catholic and of European descent like us."

Father Bernard noticed the change in his companion's visage.

"Only a few of them are true Europeans. They claim to be *españoles* and act like aristocrats by calling themselves *Don* This or *Doña* That. The rest are mongrels, of mixed blood."

"Your outlook seems rather harsh."

"Their presumptions rely solely on the land that has been passed down over a few centuries."

"The Spaniards that I have met seem so robust. To survive this frontier life must have required an unusual perseverance."

"But their spiritual and financial progress languishes. Their distrust of outsiders is second only to their envy of each other."

"You judge your flock too sternly, *prêtre*. They seem no different than people in France or any other place."

"Don't forget that our purpose here is to steer their faith on a narrow course. You need to act forcefully and with conviction."

Father Bernard refilled his goblet and took a long drink while gazing out a nearby window. He turned to his friend before resuming the conversation, "Do you remember my cousin, Lucienne?"

Father LaSalle leaned forward in thought, "Vaguely."

"My uncle had his life all planned out and raised his son under the strictest of circumstances. He would be a great engineer someday. But Luc's true ambition was different."

"I remember now. Your cousin ran off to become a sculptor. But I fail to see your point, Bernard."

He responded by walking over to refill his host's goblet which set atop a small table, "Serve our Lord with humility and compassion; otherwise the wine will always taste bitter."

Father LaSalle stared back at Father Bernard and then at the cup. He reached for his drink, but miscalculated the distance. The cup dropped to the floor; all that remained of its contents was a dull, crimson spot on the wooden floor.

Chapter Nine

Flickering candles radiated sporadic illuminations upon the fine china, crystal, and silverware. Abran gazed over his uncle's tabletop and tried to imagine the earlier *Shabbats* celebrated by his forefathers. He speculated that they might not differ much from the traditional Sunday gatherings at his parents' house. Wearing the prayer shawl and yarmulke tonight, he hoped to discover as much of his lost birthright as possible while away from his parents' house.

Don Moisés proved to be a proficient teacher. After dinner, the pair studied the journal entries, thankful for the many ancestors who recorded the meaningful events in their lives. The Jewish Bible unlocked a spiritual realm that surpassed the historical scope and stilted doctrine of the Holy Roman Empire. Together they discovered, together they debated, and together they reasoned the meaning of the Bible's passages.

Later that evening, Abran assisted *Don* Moisés with returning their religious articles into the trunk.

The events that unfolded the following Sunday caught everyone by surprise, including Father Bernard, who served as co-celebrant. Father LaSalle's homily gave no hint of what would come next. Father Bernard detected a hint of aggravation in his friend's voice. "There are two important matters that I wish to announce. First, I have decided to appoint a new *mayordomo* for this church."

The congregation reacted noisily to the shocking news. *Doña* Maria drew her hand over her mouth, while her husband crossed his arms and stared angrily ahead.

"*Señor* Espinosa failed to fulfill my expectations. Your *mayordomo* needs to serve his pastor obediently."

A great uproar followed the next proclamation, "For this reason, I have chosen Samuel Ortiz as your new *mayordomo*."

A male congregant shouted out, "*¿Cómo es posible?*"

Father Bernard caught sight of Samuel standing against the back wall. He grinned smugly, while being congratulated by a group of unsavory men. One man leaned over to shake his hand while another patted Samuel on the back.

"Silence! I did not expect my decision to be a popular one. However, you must accept it."

Father LaSalle slowly scanned the crowd until the congregation was completely quiet.

"There is a second matter. The Archbishop has decided to excommunicate Moisés Espinosa for his refusal to submit to the authority of the Church."

Father Bernard watched as *Don* Pablo buried his head in his hands; *Doña* Maria quickly slid over to comfort him. Several people shook their heads as they crossed themselves.

"*Señor* Espinosa surrenders his right to public worship or to receive the Holy Sacraments. Beware of harboring any misguided sympathies for him!"

Father Bernard believed that his *paysan* has acted unwisely, especially after having met the Espinosa family himself. He vowed never to repeat Father Pierre's foolish blunder and promised himself to act more compassionately toward his parishioners.

"Let us continue with the Celebration of the Eucharist."

The worshippers rose from their seats and started singing a devotional hymn as tears ran down the cheeks of a mute *Don* Pablo and *Doña* Maria.

Chapter Ten

Alejandro de Espinosa stood on the deck of a ship with his wife and two young sons. They waved to a group of people gathered on a pier as the ship slowly steered toward the open sea.

Today I embark on a journey to New Spain with my family. We seek an escape from the Inquisition and its many informers. I pray that our new homeland will be free of this madness.

Upon arriving in Mexico, Alejandro checked his inventory list in a ledger as *mestizo* laborers loaded small- and medium-sized crates onto oxcarts. The children played a game of "peek-a-boo" around their mother's skirts while waiting for their father.

I will ply my trade as a merchant. Our destination is the new settlement of Zacatecas where silver has been discovered. Alejandro de Espinosa. June 2, 1547.

Departing passengers moved about underneath the covered boardwalk of the newly-constructed Las Vegas train station. Periodic rumbles and hissing sounds resonated from the steam engine, which added a surreal element to the scene. *Don* Pablo, *Doña* Maria, *Don* Moisés, and Abran stood next to a passenger car as workers loaded the various luggage and crates into the freight cars,.

Don Pablo expressed his concerns, "This trip couldn't happen at a worse time. Do you have to leave now?"

"We stand to gain a lot from this journey. Besides, Abran and I hope to find some new suppliers for our stores," replied *Don* Moisés.

"But your excommunication - "

"To hell with that! The future of our business is more important than the rantings of that priest."

"We may not have much of a business left when you return."

A skeptical *Don* Moisés shook his head, "That's absurd. Do you think our *vecinos* will stop trading with us just because of him? Will they go all the way to Santa Fe for their supplies?"

"My *tío* might be right, father. Lots of people depend on us for their provisions and employment. They consider you the *patrons* of the village," observed Abran.

"But they might fear the priest too much."

Doña Maria reached for her husband's arm, "Pablo, let's be more patient. After all, the bonds we share with the people in the valley go back many generations."

Several blasts of the train's whistle signaled the passengers to start boarding. *Don* Moisés patted his brother on the back, "You have a clever wife, *hermano*."

"I suppose we'll find out soon enough. Abran, you need to devote some serious thought toward your situation."

Abran shuffled nervously. *Doña* Maria released her husband's arm and reached out for her son's hand, "*Hijo*, you stand to lose the most because you're young. Don't be foolish."

A protracted whistle sounded and a bell started ringing steadily from atop the engine. A conductor shouted out, "All aboard! Passenger service to Dodge City, Topeka, and Kansas City is now boarding."

Doña Maria and *Don* Pablo began exchanging hugs with Abran and *Don* Moisés before they boarded the train. Stopping in front of the passenger car's entry, *Don* Moisés turned around for one final goodbye. *Doña* Maria crossed herself before shouting out, "*¡Vaya con Dios!*"

The trip to Kansas City, which turned monotonous at times, revealed new wonders to Abran. Mountains and endless prairie passed by at an astonishing rate. His uncle pointed out many landmarks from his days on the Santa Fe Trail and regaled Abran with stories of the frontier towns and diverse people he encountered. Soon, it was difficult to distinguish one Kansas rail town from another. But Kansas City proved to be the most fascinating of any of them including Topeka, the railroad's headquarters. The sheer size and commotion was incredible for Abran to behold, as was the Missouri River whose breadth dwarfed the entire Rio Sagrado Valley at its widest point.

After they checked into a hotel, *Don* Moisés and Abran explored the thriving city hoping to expand their supplier network over the next four days. Abran observed his uncle's interactions with the *americanos*, some of whom spoke English with unusual accents, and analyzed each outcome since this responsibility would someday fall upon him. However, a few surreptitious contacts were made for purposes other than the family business.

The following morning, *Don* Moisés and Abran found themselves in front of Isaac Cohen's Tailor Shop. Rabbi Cohen noticed the two unfamiliar men while straightening some fabric on a large counter. The older man held an indistinguishable parcel under his left arm. A rusty door hinge squeaked as the men opened the door; an unusual metallic piece brushed against a hanging bell that signaled their entry. The strangers studied the bell for a moment – the older man said something inaudible which elicited a laugh from the younger one.

Rabbi Cohen approached the pair, "Gentlemen, how may I help you?"

Don Moisés retrieved a piece of paper from his vest pocket and struggled with the proper pronunciation, "We are looking for *Izak*, I-sock Coh-hen."

The proprietor smiled momentarily, "I am Isaac Cohen."

Don Moisés extended his right hand, Rabbi Cohen reciprocated. "My name is Moisés Espinosa. This is my nephew, Abran Espinosa."

Abran shook hands with him as well, "*Con mucho gusto*, I mean I am pleased to meet you, sir."

"I welcome you both. Your manner of speech tells me that you might be visiting from someplace different."

"New Mexico. We have a family business there," replied *Don* Moisés.

"How may I serve you?"

"One of the business owners we visited suggested that we talk to you. Are you a Jewish priest?"

The stranger's question caught Rabbi Cohen by surprise. He stroked his beard for a few seconds before he responded cautiously, "Who mentioned me to you?"

Don Moisés consulted the piece of paper again, "Mr. Goldberg. He owns the glassware factory."

"Chaim Goldberg? He is a member of our new congregation. But gentlemen, I am a rabbi, a teacher of God's Law."

"You are the head of your Jewish church, yes?"

"I lead the worship services and study God's Laws and Teachings. The Jewish ways are different than the Christian churches. Why are you so interested in finding me?"

Don Moisés walked over to the countertop, set the parcel down, and uncovered it. He placed the Bible and journal next to each other. "My nephew and I discovered these. It seems that our Spanish ancestors were Jews. We need someone to teach us the Jewish ways."

Rabbi Cohen studied the books for a few moments, "This one appears to be a Bible, but what is this other book?"

"It is a family journal that dates back to 1492 when the Jews were expelled from Spain."

"Fascinating, I have heard about your people."

Abran placed his hand on the Rabbi's shirtsleeve, "Then you'll help us?"

The young man's abrupt manner startled the rabbi; he involuntarily backed away to gather his thoughts. None of his academic or spiritual training had prepared him for this event. His spiritual knowledge was limited to the world of the *Ashkenazi*, the Jews of Germany and Eastern Europe, and simple matters like one is either a Jew or not a Jew. Now he faced a divine conundrum.

"I am not sure how our congregation would react if they find out about this. They are Jewish by birth and tradition."

"But we are Jewish by birth. We have been robbed of our tradition through no fault of our own," responded *Don* Moisés.

Rabbi Cohen walked over to the front of the window and stared out at the bustling street. Perhaps he could consent to their request as a *mitzvah*, an act of human kindness.

"How long will you be here?"

"Three more days. We are locating suppliers for our mercantile stores back home."

"There is only so much that I can teach you, but I am willing to try. Can you spare two to three hours every day?"

"Of course. What time should we arrive?"

"My afternoons are slow sometimes. How about two o'clock this afternoon?"

"Wonderful. Thank you, Mister Cohen."

Abran inspected a suit that hung on a nearby rack. He gently fingered the fabric and looked back at the rabbi, "There is something that I would like to ask you."

"Yes?"

"Would you make my wedding suit?"

"I would be honored."

"Could you measure me now?"

Don Moisés scolded his nephew, "Abran, I'm sure Mister Cohen has other business to tend to right now."

The rabbi pointed to a small, raised platform near the counter, "It is no bother at all. Step up here while I get my tape measure."

Normally, the return trip would have been a tedious affair, but with the benefits secured by *Don* Moisés and Abran, it was a pleasant, exhilarating journey. An expanded line of merchandise ensured a brighter future while the new suppliers welcomed the opportunities to expand and diversify their markets. But most importantly, Rabbi Cohen had provided them with welcome insights and wisdom that they never dreamt possible. The generous rabbi filled a spiritual void that would provide a direction for their future pursuits.

Abran carried a small crate out of the rear storeroom just as a bell rung. *Don* Tomás and Isabella stood in the doorway and stared up at the bell that hung overhead; it was identical to the one in Rabbi Cohen's shop. They exchanged a puzzled look before proceeding inside. Even though *Don* Moisés was busy assisting a customer at the front counter, he acknowledged *Don* Tomás' presence with a nod.

Don Tomás and Isabella approached Abran; Abran and Isabella shared a deferential glance. After everyone exchanged cordial pleasantries, *Don* Tomás handed his daughter a shopping list. Isabella excused herself from the men's presence.

"Can we talk somewhere more private?" asked *Don* Tomás.

"The storeroom?"

Don Tomás nodded in agreement and followed Abran. *Don* Tomás remained standing but motioned for Abran to sit on a nearby crate, "My wife and I are worried about the wedding. Do you plan to make amends with Father LaSalle?"

Abran jumped up, "What am I supposed to do, *Don* Tomás? He embarrassed me in front of the whole village."

"Abran, there is little time left."

Abran started pacing back and forth, "I love Isabella with all my heart, but I resent having to submit to that -"

"Sometimes we have to sacrifice our pride which can be difficult."

"But there are other considerations."

"Are they important enough to risk losing Isabella?"

Abran sat back down and stared at his folded hands. It took several seconds for him to weigh his options. "If only that priest and Samuel Ortiz had kept their noses out of our business."

Don Tomás attempted to ease Abran's anguish by placing a reassuring hand on the young man's shoulder. After a prolonged pause, Abran faced *Don* Tomás, "I will talk to the priest after Sunday Mass."

"Good. This is a step in the right direction."

"But I still don't trust him."

"I'm sure everything will turn out well."

Abran stood up and walked over to a small table. He picked up an ornate box and returned to *Don* Tomás, "*Con tu permiso*, I would like to give this to Isabella."

A glance at the label revealed some scrolled text, "Schwartz's Hat Shop, Kansas City, Missouri."

"Certainly."

The men exited the storeroom. *Don* Tomás relieved Isabella of the supplies and directed her toward Abran. Abran glanced around the store before speaking, "*Buenos dias,* my beloved. I've missed you so much."

"I missed you, *mí cariño.* Did your trip go well?"

"Yes it did. I brought you a surprise."

Abran offered the box to Isabella. Her face registered a look of delight as she removed the hat, "Abran, this is so beautiful."

"Not as beautiful as you."

Isabella blushed as Abran gently placed the hat on her head. She turned toward the front counter where *Don* Tomás and *Don* Moisés were busy conducting business. She leaned over and kissed her intended on the cheek, "Thank you. How did your meeting with my father go?"

"Good. I plan on talking to Father LaSalle after Sunday Mass."

"I will pray to our Blessed Mother and ask her to soften the *padre's* heart."

"I'm not sure that will work, Isa."

Isabella continued to admire the hat after removing it. Abran assisted her as she placed it back into the box – she delicately brushed his hand with her fingertips. "When are you and Clemente riding to Los Pinos?"

"*Mañana*. We'll return on Saturday after delivering supplies to our *vaqueros*."

"I wish I was the one going with you."

"That is a tempting thought my love, and a scandalous one."

Abran crossed himself and drew his hands together in mock piety which elicited a giggle from Isabella. *Don* Tomás beckoned Isabella to join him at the front counter.

"Take care, my beloved. And thank you for this beautiful gift."

"You're welcome, Isa."

Isabella proudly displayed her gift to the men; *Don* Tomás cradled the hat in his hands, nodded approvingly, and returned the hat to his daughter. "*Qué bonita, mi hija.*"

Don Moisés commented, "It's perfect, Isabella. I was with my nephew when he chose it."

Don Tomás and Isabella gathered up their provisions and headed for the door. They both turned to Abran and bid their farewells before leaving. *Don* Moisés motioned for Abran to join him at the front counter the second that the Luceros were out the door. Over the next few minutes, Abran updated his uncle on the just concluded conversation and his decision to meet with the priest.

Chapter Eleven

High above the timberline of the Sangre de Cristo Mountains, snow-fed lakes and natural springs formed the headwaters of the Rio Sagrado. Countless small creeks flowed down from the high country and converged into larger streams that meandered through lush meadows and pine forests. The small, steep canyons broadened where the various tributaries merged. Small communities like Cañoncito, created by the division of land grants within the same families, prospered because of the Upper Rio Sagrado's rich pastures. Farming became the predominant livelihood where the valley widened just above the village of Rio Sagrado, and within the many communities downstream.

Eventually the Rio Sagrado wandered past the once-prosperous, abandoned pueblo of Cícuye, through the village of San Miguel del Vado, the crossing point of the Santa Fe Trail, then south toward the village of Anton Chico and through the vast, featureless plains of southeastern New Mexico named the Llano Estacado, or the Staked Plains, by the first Spanish explorers. Some nine hundred miles from its source, the Rio Sagrado merged with the Rio Grande southeast of the Big Bend.

Halfway to Los Pinos, Abran and Clemente pitched camp near a beaver pond. They had learned long ago that the tranquility of a beaver pond made slumber much easier than camping next to the flowing river. The countless stars shone brightly overhead in the black sky despite the roaring campfire that Clemente had built to fend off the brisk night air. After they set aside their tin plates and utensils, Abran filled a tin cup with whiskey and passed the bottle to his companion. He stared pensively into the fire while Clemente filled his cup, "Cleme, would you promise to keep a secret if I shared something important with you?"

"You have my word, *primo*."

"My uncle and I found a book that was written by many of my ancestors. It was hidden in an old trunk that belonged to my grandfather."

"That's amazing, but what's so mysterious about that?"

"We found out from the book that we are the descendants of Spanish Jews. *Somos judíos*, Cleme."

"But isn't that a bad thing? Could you go to hell for that?"

"That's what the Church wants everyone to believe."

"But why should you care about this? You're a Catholic just like me."

Abran paused to stir the fire with a stick, "Cleme, are you proud to be an *español*?"

"Why do you ask such a foolish question?"

"Well, my pride includes being a Jew. We lived in Spain long before Christ was born."

"What happened? Why aren't there any Jewish churches here?"

"The Catholic rulers forced the Jews to leave Spain and abandon their wealth. The ones who stayed became converts, but some of them chose to secretly practice their true faith. We've been hiding ever since then."

"So the *chingadera* between your uncle and the priest is over this?"

Abran nodded his head, Clemente continued, "But *Padre* LaSalle thinks your uncle is a *brujo*. Wouldn't it be better if he knew the truth?"

"That would be worse. The Church accuses us of killing Christ. People have been blaming the Jews for something that was going to happen anyway."

"This is ridiculous, Abran. When the *americanos* arrived, they brought those other religions with them."

"Yes, but those religions also came from Europe. The Archbishop won't try to do anything against the *gringo* churches. It's easier for the Church to harass the Jews in Spain, in Mexico, or wherever they find them."

The two *compañeros* refilled their cups and drank heartily. Clemente took a moment to ponder Abran's dilemma.

"So what should I do, Cleme? I have to meet with the priest when we return."

"Do you fear that pompous bastard?"

"I don't trust him. Part of me is willing to do whatever he asks so I can marry Isabella. But I also want to continue being a Jew. My heart is so confused. I shouldn't have to hide my real faith."

Clemente diverted his attention to the fire and placed another log on it. He continued to stare into the fire for several seconds before he responded, "When your Jewish ancestors pretended to be Catholic, what did they call themselves?"

Abran thought back to the earliest journal entries, "They were called *conversos*. Why do you ask?"

"That is what you will become. You'll continue being a Catholic and deceive whomever you have to so you can be with Isa."

"Do I deceive Isa, too?"

"Perhaps she will agree to join your scheme. I think she loves you enough to do that."

"But - "

"You have to do this! Your destiny is to be a *converso*, maybe it will be your children's destiny as well."

"How long do we keep hiding?"

"*¿Quién sabe?* Just look at all the changes around here – the arrival of the *gringos* and the railroad. Maybe someday there will be no more hiding in fear or shame."

Abran felt the effects of the whiskey and tried to clear his head by taking several deep breaths of the cool mountain air. The solution to his dilemma was there all along thanks to *Don* Solomon and his contemporaries who risked everything with their duplicity. He knew that if he implemented this strategy it would be complicated and risky. But he also knew that he could depend on *Don* Moisés and Clemente's help. He wanted to pray for Isabella's cooperation, but his intoxicated mind wasn't sure if this was a Catholic or a Jewish matter. Abran chose to postpone this question until the morning.

As he watched Clemente tend to the fire, Abran barely managed to crawl into his bedroll before he succumbed to the many hours in the saddle, the 8000-foot elevation, and the past two day's anxiety.

Chapter Twelve

As arranged, Abran and his parents met with Father LaSalle after Sunday Mass. While the Espinosas sat in the front pew of the sanctuary, the priest reviewed a list of requirements that Abran would have to meet before he returned to the church in good standing. He then launched into a lengthy diatribe against unholy behavior and alliances. Finally, the conference appeared to draw to a conclusion when Father LaSalle queried Abran, "Do you understand my conditions?"

Abran glanced at his parents before responding, "Yes Father."

"How soon will you be moving back into your parent's house?"

"This afternoon."

"You agree to limit your contacts with your uncle to business matters only?"

Abran nodded.

"You also agree to assist Samuel Ortiz with whatever tasks I assign?"

Abran hesitated momentarily, which prompted *Don* Pablo to express his concern, "*Padre,* you must not permit Samuel to abuse his authority over my son."

Father LaSalle's posture stiffened, "I have every confidence in *Señor* Ortiz."

Don Pablo bowed his head while the priest awaited Abran's response.

"I agree, Father."

"You will report to me every weekday afternoon for an hour

of religious instruction."

Abran nodded again. Father LaSalle turned toward his parents, "Do you agree to these conditions, *Señor* and *Señora* Espinosa?"

Doña Maria deferred her response and turned toward her husband who answered for both of them, "We agree, Father."

"Very well. I expect strict adherence to our agreement."

Doña Maria crossed herself. Father LaSalle unfurled a sash-like garment from his sleeves and draped it around his neck. He stepped into the main aisle and extended his right arm toward the rear of the church. "Let us seal this pact through the Sacrament of Penance."

Abran's head bolted up, "But I – "

Doña Maria stealthily jabbed her son's ribs with her elbow. Abran concealed his blunder by clearing his throat before standing up, "I understand, Father." He followed the priest to the confessional.

Don Pablo faced his wife, "If Samuel dares to lay a finger... "

Doña Maria tenderly placed a finger over her husband's lips, "*Cállate, hombre.* Let us pray for the children's wedding."

The couple crossed themselves as they knelt down to implore the Lord's blessing on this matter.

On the first day of his assigned chores, Abran found himself in the churchyard with Samuel Ortiz, who pointed to some weeds while handing Abran a hoe. As Abran started clearing the weeds, Samuel moved a chair to a shady spot, sat down, and tipped the chair back against the rectory wall. He positioned his hat over his eyes and dozed off. A disgusted Abran shook his head while cursing under his breath.

Abran continued to work when Father LaSalle emerged from the rectory. The priest acknowledged Abran's presence with a nod and looked around for Samuel. Abran silently pointed toward Samuel who was concealed by a woodpile. An annoyed Father LaSalle approached Samuel and nudged the back legs of the chair with his foot. This startled the laggard and caused him to tip over. As Samuel clumsily scrambled to his feet, the priest loudly admonished his *mayordomo*, who contritely hurried toward the remaining gardening tools. After Father LaSalle departed, an irate Samuel directed an epithet toward Abran as he dusted himself off. Abran smugly smiled back and returned to his task.

The two week ordeal finally drew to a close. From everything Abran reported, *Don* Moisés was amazed by his nephew's resilience in dealing with the obnoxious priest and outmaneuvering Samuel Ortiz. The following Sunday found Abran and his parents waiting their turn for Communion. Everything went smoothly for Abran, which eased the congregants' apprehensions. Upon returning to their seats, *Doña* Maria proudly turned to Abran and gently squeezed his hand after they returned to their seats.

Isabella sat at one end of a kitchen table lost in thought – she wiped away a tear with her right hand. She had just met with Abran at their secret location and learned of Abran's secret endeavors and of the journal's contents. She imagined the look of bewilderment on her face as Abran punctuated his words with animated gestures.

Doña Nicolasa noticed her daughter's distress upon entering the room and placed her hands on Isabella's head, *"Hija mía,* why are you so sad?"

Isabella struggled for a response. *Doña* Nicolasa sat down in an adjacent chair and cradled her daughter's hands with her own. "Tell me what is wrong, Isa."

"It, it's about Abran, Mama."

"Is he hurt or sick?"

"No, nothing like that."

As *Doña* Nicolasa awaited more information, Isabella became more distraught. "I found out about the strange dealings between him and *Don* Moisés. Abran wanted to share this with me before the wedding."

Doña Nicolasa learned of their secret meetings when she overheard her younger children talking about it last year. She chose not to interfere since she felt that the two young adults, as eldest children in their respective families, could be trusted to avoid any imprudent behavior. "What could be so bad, *hija?*"

"They found out from an old book that they are Jews. They both want to continue practicing in secret," Isabella buried her face in her hands, "This is terrible! I love Abran so much, but I don't know what to do now."

Her mother wiped the tears from her own eyes and carefully prepared her reply. *Doña* Nicolasa folded her hands together in a prayerful pose before she turned toward her daughter, "You will do the same thing that your father has done all these years, Isa."

"Mama, what are you telling me?"

"Your father loved me so much that he accepted what I am. We agreed to keep this to ourselves. I have kept a few of the practices that I was raised with."

"But... the Church."

"Our Jewish heritage goes back a long way. You have no reason to be ashamed of Abran and *Don* Moisés. Besides, there are many families here in Rio Sagrado who share our history."

"So am I Jewish or Catholic?"

"You are Catholic out of necessity."

"This is all so confusing. What about Papa?"

"We knew that the day might come when we might have to tell our children. We'd rather expose you to everything I know and let you decide how you want to deal with this."

"So I can still marry Abran?"

"Oh yes. There is no doubt in my mind that your special connection will strengthen your marriage."

"What about Father LaSalle?"

"We'll let him keep thinking that our valley is full of *brujas* and *brujos*."

The comment elicited a laugh from her daughter. Isabella rose from her chair and knelt next to her mother. *Doña* Nicolasa cradled her daughter's head in her hands and kissed her forehead, "Don't worry, everything will be alright. We'll spend some special time together these next few days."

Chapter Thirteen

Luis de Espinosa had departed Zacatecas, Mexico, in September, 1695, with his young wife and three oxcarts of personal belongings and trade goods. They journeyed north to El Paso del Norte and then onwards through the unforgiving, parched land referred to as *El Jornada del Muerto*. This somber reference, Journey of the Dead Man, resulted from the crude, hastily-dug graves that increased with each expedition along the rugged path that followed the Rio Grande northwards from El Paso to Socorro.

We leave Zacatecas on this day, September 6, 1695, to journey north to the frontier. We are part of a group organized by Juan Paez Hurtado and follow Don Diego de Vargas in his efforts to reclaim the lost kingdom. Some of our Jewish brothers and sisters travel with us. We hope to transplant our celebrations like El Dia Grande and the Feast of Esther to a new land.

We have been told to expect a harsh and dangerous journey. But like my ancestors, the promise of a new homeland outweighs whatever perils and hardships lie ahead. Our new settlement will allow us to practice our faith away from prying eyes. Our unborn children deserve this opportunity to reclaim their lost heritage. Luis de Espinosa.

The long-awaited day had finally arrived. *Doña* Nicolasa revealed all that she could about her Sephardic faith as they made the wedding preparations. Isabella grew less apprehensive with each passing day and welcomed the clandestine meeting between *Doña* Nicolasa, Abran, and herself a week before the wedding day. *Doña* Nicolasa's surprising revelation and blessing caught Abran by surprise at first, but served to strengthen the young couple's resolve.

Father LaSalle led a traditional wedding procession toward the church on a beautiful summer morning. The same six musicians from the church dedication followed the priest, while playing a lively tune. *Don* Tomás, Isabella, and *Doña* Nicolasa trailed the musicians followed by *Don* Pablo, Abran, and *Doña* Maria. The best man and maid of honor, Clemente and Agapita, walked ahead of the remaining relatives and friends who would fill the church beyond its capacity.

The Lucero and Espinosa families spared little expense in decorating the outside and inside of the church. Two ornate chairs and kneeling benches specially crafted for the occasion accentuated what would be referred to as "the wedding of all weddings" in Rio Sagrado for many years.

After the ceremony, the entourage made its way to the Lucero *hacienda*. The wedding guests lined up in front of the main entrance, while the main party retreated inside for a brief respite. Three railroad surveyors of Irish descent had formed a kinship with the Espinosas by virtue of their Catholic faith and spirited personas. After he caught sight of them, *Don* Miguel escorted them to the front of the line as a special favor to *Don* Pablo.

Patrick Flanagan, Seamus O'Riley, and Michael Sullivan extended their heartfelt wishes to the wedding party before being led to one of the many benches that lined the perimeter of a large room. They noticed the two large tables occupying the center of the room were laden with pastries, wine, and whiskey. Eventually, *Don* Miguel and *Doña* Emilia directed the trio to the tables and sat with them as they snacked on some pastries.

Patrick Flanagan delighted in one particular item, "These cookies are delicious. What was it you called them?"

"*Bizcochitos,*" replied *Don* Miguel.

Seamus O'Riley joined in, "I've never tasted anything like these. Thank you for the hospitality."

"Indeed, Mr. Valencia. This is quite a shindig. Abran and his bride make a fetching couple. Reminds me a bit of the festive weddings back home in Ireland," added Michael Sullivan.

"It is my pleasure, gentleman."

A server presented a tray filled with steaming cups. *Don* Miguel encouraged the men to sample the beverage, "This is a special drink that we call *la merienda.*"

The looked at each other for a brief moment before Patrick spoke, "Hot cocoa, perhaps?"

"Hot cocoa flavored with cinnamon. It is a ceremonial drink brought up from Mexico. I think it originated with the *Aztecas.*"

Doña Emilia joined in, "No wedding would be complete without *la merienda, señores.*"

Seamus inquired after taking a second sip, "By the way, I haven't caught sight of *Don* Moisés. Where is he?"

Don Miguel looked over to his wife before speaking, "He will show up later."

"Is there a problem?"

The men followed *Don* Miguel's gaze toward Father LaSalle and noticed the dour look on the priest's face. He sat with his arms folded and showed little interest in the festivities.

"*Don* Moisés and our new priest don't get along very well. He'll show up once the priest leaves."

"I know what you mean. The good father hasn't exactly welcomed our lads with open arms on Sunday mornings," commented Michael.

"Your *padre* looks like he could use a shot of that whiskey," observed Seamus.

He walked over to the table, poured two glasses of whiskey, and offered one of them to Father LaSalle. The priest refused the drink with a dismissive wave of his right hand. Seamus returned to his seat and offered the glass to *Don* Miguel, while shaking his head in disbelief. Before he took a hearty drink from his glass, the Irishman expressed his shock, "Imagine that, a priest who don't drink whiskey. What's this world come to?"

A short time later, the wedding guests dined on a lavish meal. Abran and Isabella radiated with happiness while a steady stream of conversation and laughter filled the large patio. Although the Irishmen reveled in the joyous celebration, they felt a twinge of longing for their families back in Kansas. They watched as Father LaSalle excused himself from the head table; very few attendees acknowledged his departure. His place at the head table was quickly cleared and a new place setting was added.

The entourage extended an energetic greeting when *Don* Moisés made his entrance a short time later. After he exchanged pleasantries with those seated at the head table, *Don* Moisés poured a glass of wine and raised it aloft. "I apologize for my late arrival. I offer a loving tribute to Abran and Isabella on their joyous union. *¡Salud!*"

The crowd returned the salutation. *Don* Moisés refilled his glass and stared at the wine before raising his glass once again, "This wine brings pleasure only to those who seek it. Pity the man who finds it distasteful. *Para mis vecinos... ¡Salud!*"

A boisterous response follows. "*¡Salud!*"

Don Moisés sat down and dined with gusto. Michael turned to his mates and commented, "Makes you wonder, don't it boys?"

Chapter Fourteen

A raised, wooden platform served as a dance floor, while gaily decorated tables and benches bordered its perimeter. The first song performed by the musicians was the traditional "*La Marcha.*", an intricate, communal procession involving the wedding party and guests. Several dances later, Abran and Isabella made a quick getaway to recover from an already overwhelming day. Abran leaned over and kissed Isabella on the cheek, "What a day this has been, my beloved."

"It is like a dream come true, Abran. We are so blessed to have our family and friends." She returned Abran's kiss, "Your sacrifice made this all possible. Thank you."

"Isa, I can't live my life without you."

"All my prayers were answered. Did you pray for us during this madness?"

Abran noticed that Isabella was clutching a gold crucifix hanging from her neck. "Yes, but maybe not the same way you did."

Isabella placed her index finger on Abran's lips. "We must be careful with our words and thoughts, *cariño.*"

Clemente and Agapita approached the couple; there is no doubt in Isabella's mind that their betrothal would soon follow. Clemente beckoned to the newlyweds.

"It's time to do more dancing. *¡Vamanos!*"

Isabella reached down and rubbed her left heel. "*Aye,* Cleme. My feet hurt so much from these tight slippers."

Agapita rolled her eyes. "You two are already acting like *viejitos.* Come on."

Clemente and Agapita stood their ground and beckoned with outstretched hands. Clemente winked as he spoke, "No excuses now. You'll have plenty of time to recuperate later tonight."

Abran and Isabella shared a defeated look as they rose from their chairs. Abran paired up with Agapita, while Isabella joined Clemente on the dance floor. The musicians struck up a lively waltz.

Two hours later, the foursome made their way to Abran and Isabella's new house. Clemente stopped the buggy and held up a lantern while Abran lit another one. The lanterns' soft radiance revealed the front door and door frames festooned with ribbons of various widths and colors. The bride and groom smiled wearily at each other. Abran hugged Clemente while Isabella leaned over to kiss her sister on the cheek.

The newlyweds entered their abode, which left Clemente and Agapita alone. They embraced briefly and stared at the shut door before they climbed aboard the buggy to return to the Lucero home.

The lantern's flickering revealed Isabella's wedding-night nervousness. Abran attempted to ease his beloved's anxiety as he approached a wash basin that set on a nearby night stand. Abran dipped a cloth into the basin and wrung it out. He sensuously wiped Isabella's face and lightly kissed where the cloth had touched her. The cloth was immersed and wrung out again. This time Abran wiped and kissed Isabella's neck, first on one side, then on the other.

Shortly afterwards, Isabella reached for the cloth and returned the favor. The invigorated couple embraced after shedding their wedding garments and shuffled slowly toward the bed. The passion overwhelmed Isabella to the point of almost losing consciousness; Abran lifted her into his arms at the critical moment and gently deposited her on the down mattress. He climbed in beside her and made love to her for the first time. Like most passionate novices their lovemaking was awkward and hurried, but nonetheless exhilarating.

Chapter Fifteen

Pristine snow had blanketed everything in sight, the result of an unseasonal snowfall that signaled the arrival of an early winter. A pregnant Isabella stepped outside with a steaming cup of coffee as Abran tossed newly-cut firewood into a pile at one end of the porch. Abran marveled at her stunning beauty accentuated by the red calico dress sewn by her mother's expert hand and the white woolen shawl wrapped around her shoulders. Abran moved toward his wife and drank the coffee from one hand while wrapping the other around her protruding abdomen. As they gazed out at the serene setting, Abran reflected back to an earlier time and a journal entry that made him appreciate his ancestor's resolve.

Luis De Espinosa first built a simple adobe house and a small store whose interior was lined with crude wooden shelves. Over time, the structures expanded with his children's births and his enterprise's fortunes. The *Camino Real*, the trade route between Santa Fe and Durango, Mexico, served as a vital link to his continued success.

Our short wait in Santa Fe is finally over following our contentious and near-disastrous expedition from El Paso del Norte. We have arrived with our compañeros to this beautiful valley nourished by the Rio Sagrado. We are thankful to be here and count our blessings.

This divine valley offers us so many opportunities. The fertile land near the river should produce good crops. Our cattle have plenty of grassland above the village. The nearby Sangre de Cristo Mountains offer abundant timber. Like my forefathers, I will trade goods with my neighbors. My devoted wife and I hope

*that our hard work will build a promising future for our unborn
children and the generations that follow.*

*There is much to hope for with the founding of our new
settlement. Perhaps this new land is our reward for the dangers
faced by my Jewish ancestors. Luis De Espinosa. June 24, 1696.*

Doña Nicolasa and a local midwife tended to Isabella as
she struggled to give birth. Meanwhile, Abran paced nervously
about the kitchen while *Doña* Maria stirred the embers inside
the wood stove. Isabella's muffled groans from the adjoining
bedroom unnerved her mate while *Don* Pablo and *Don* Tomás
calmly sat at the table sipping their coffee.

"Why is this taking so damn long?"

Doña Maria tried to calm her son, "Patience, *hijo*. This is
Isabella's first time to give birth."

"But it sounds like she's in a lot of pain."

"She's in some pain, but it is all part of the miracle."

Doña Nicolasa called out to *Doña* Maria who promptly
departed. Abran stared at the closed door and then turned to
his elders.

"Is something wrong?"

Don Tomás pointed to a vacant chair, "Abran, sit down and
relax."

"I can't. All I can think about is Uncle Moisés' wife, Elena.
Both her and the baby ended up dying."

Don Pablo and *Don* Tomás bowed their heads for a moment
while crossing themselves. *Don* Pablo beckoned his son to
the table, "Those things happen for reasons only God knows.
Isabella is in good hands."

Abran sat down and positioned himself at the edge of the
chair, "How can you be so calm at a time like this?"

"*Hijo*, I was just as nervous when you were born, but I
learned to be patient," replied *Don* Pablo.

"It doesn't seem fair, father. We men have the easy part, *verdad*?"

Don Pablo directed a knowing glance at *Don* Tomás before responding, "The first child is a trial from God... and a blessing. A father's hope for the future rests on his firstborn child."

Don Tomás joined in, "Providing us with children is God's way of sending us comfort. You have nothing to worry about."

A high-pitched, diminutive cry was followed by female voices exclaiming their delight. Abran looked anxiously at the two men and started to rise from his chair. *Don* Pablo detained him with a firm hand grip, "Wait, this time belongs to the women. Your turn will soon come."

Abran protested and tried to resist his father's grasp, "But I'm the father."

Don Pablo maintained his hand hold, "Right now, you're only the father."

"What do you mean, only the father?"

"Only another woman who has given birth knows what Isabella has endured. Let the *viejitas* fuss over the new mother and baby for the time being."

Don Tomás rose from his seat, approached the stove, and poured a cup of coffee which he handed to Abran.

Doña Maria entered the room carrying a bundle of soiled linens and deposited them in an empty washtub. She turned to the three men and announced, "Isabella and the baby are fine. They'll be ready in a few minutes." She walked over to the table and leaned over to hug Abran first, then her husband, "It's a boy, a handsome, healthy boy."

The men celebrated with handshakes and embraces. *Don* Pablo could hardly contain himself, "Congratulations, *hijo*. This is a happy moment for all of us."

He hugged his now sobbing wife one more time, "Our first grandchild, Maria. Can you believe it?"

"God has blessed us, Pablo."

Doña Nicolasa summoned Abran who quickly raced into the bedroom. A slightly disheveled Isabella was propped up in the bed – the bundled newborn rested on her chest. *Doña* Nicolasa and the midwife excused themselves and exited the bedroom as Abran approached his wife and son.

He leaned down to kiss her while brushing a wayward wisp of hair with the back of his hand, "How are you doing, my beloved?"

"Very tired... but happy."

"You were in labor for such a long time. I was very worried."

Isabella smiled feebly before she handed the infant to Abran, "Our son decided to be stubborn like his father."

"He's so beautiful, Isa. Thank you for giving me this son to love."

An eager *Don* Pablo and *Don* Tomás stood in the doorway. "May we see our grandson?" queried *Don* Tomás.

"Yes, come in and greet little Juan Pablo," replied Abran.

The elders approached and commented on the child's handsome features. *Don* Pablo traced the Sign of the Cross on the newborn's forehead with his thumb while *Don* Tomás kissed Isabella's hand. *Don* Pablo faced Abran and Isabella, "I thank you for naming this special child after my father and me."

Isabella smiled warmly at her father-in-law, "You're welcome, *Don* Pablo. He carries an honorable name."

Abran turned to *Don* Tomás, "Don't worry, *abuelito*, the next grandson will bear your name."

The men's sudden laughter startled the baby. The squirming bundle made Abran somewhat uncomfortable, which Isabella found amusing.

"Give him here, Papa. He should be ready for his first feeding."

Abran returned the child to Isabella after their fathers graciously excused themselves. He paused at the door, "Do you want me to send in the proud *abuelitas*?"

Isabella nodded. Abran returned and affectionately stroked her cheek. He cupped the baby's head in the palm of his hand and kissed Juan Pablo's forehead.

"*Te amo*, Isa. *Te amo*, Juan Pablo."

Chapter Sixteen

A few weeks later, Juan Pablo was baptized in the new church by Father LaSalle. *Don* Pablo and *Doña* Maria served as his proud godparents. This event preceded a duplicitous journey to Kansas City by *Don* Moisés, Abran, and Isabella. Their simple act of faith would inadvertently set off a chain of events that would affect the whole village.

Don Moisés finished recording an entry when Abran entered the house and called for his uncle, "*Tio*, where are you?"

"Here in the study."

Abran noticed the valise and suitcase setting next to *Don* Moisés, "*¿Estás listo?*"

Don Moisés cleaned his quill pen and placed the family journal under some other books on his table.

Abran registered his concern, "Shouldn't you put that in grandfather's trunk?"

"It's safe here, Abran. Who would want to take an old book like this?"

"Are you sure, *tio?*"

Don Moisés reached down for his valise and suitcase, "You worry too much, *sobrino*. Let's go see our friends in Kansas City."

Father LaSalle queried Samuel Ortiz the next afternoon in the church's sacristy about *Don* Moisés' absence from the village. Samuel was only too eager to provide details.

"Him and his nephew went on the railroad to that big city. Abran's wife and baby went with them."

This aroused the priest's suspicions, "For what reason?"

"Store business. They have been buying some of their goods there."

Father LaSalle adjusted the sleeves on his frock, "I want you to gain entry into *Don* Moisés' house and look for anything unusual. Search carefully for an odd book or unusual items."

"And if I find something?"

"Bring it to me so I can inspect it. Can you do this without drawing attention to yourself?"

"*Si, padre.* You can depend on me."

The priest locked in on Samuel's eyes and issued a firm, unmistakable directive, "You are not to take anything else, understood?"

A humiliated Samuel Ortiz could only stare back.

"Very well. Let's lock up and be on our way."

The trip to Kansas City went well and the elated trio returned to Rio Sagrado concealing a secret that would be shared only with *Doña* Nicolasa. Thanks to Rabbi Cohen's support, a *brit milah* was conducted for the newborn. His Hebrew name, Solomon ben Avraham, was chosen by Abran and Isabella.

But the joy was short-lived when *Don* Moisés discovered his books strewn over the desktop after entering his house. As he rummaged through the pile, he suddenly realized that the journal was the only book missing. *Don* Moisés quickly stormed out of his house and headed toward the corral to saddle his horse.

One of the village's eyesores was a *cantina* that was operated by Samuel Ortiz's brother, Raul. It was a notorious watering hole, misleadingly named *La Paloma*, whose rundown appearance and equally unkempt patrons discouraged prying eyes. Even the local constable, Gregorio Lopez, had learned to steer clear of this hangout when at all possible. Instead, he waited to get the drop on the criminals who frequented the *cantina* after they departed the premises in a drunken stupor. It was rumored that most of the valley's criminal doings were hatched here with the blessings of Raul and Samuel Ortiz, who profited from the stolen goods and cattle.

Samuel and two slovenly companions sat on a bench under the portal while they shared a bottle of rotgut. The sound of hoof beats captured their attention. *Don* Moisés galloped up and dismounted before any of the men could react. He grabbed a stunned Samuel by the collar and pinned him against the wall. Samuel's companions recovered their senses and stepped toward *Don* Moisés, but were discouraged by the large knife in his right hand.

"Step away, *desgraciados*. This is between me and this thieving bastard!"

They retreated as *Don* Moisés tightened his grip on Samuel's throat, "You're the one who took it, weren't you? Where is it?"

"I don't know what you're talking about."

Samuel realized that he is in serious peril when *Don* Moisés flashed the knife blade flashes before his eyes. In a perverse way, Samuel marveled at *Don* Moisés' strength and resolve, it was enough to keep his usually dependable cohorts at bay.

"Don't insult me or try my patience! You're the only one stupid enough to trespass on my property."

Samuel struggled to breathe, "The priest has it... he put me up to it."

"Damn him." *Don* Moisés spun around harshly and sent Samuel sprawling to the ground after releasing his prey. *Don* Moisés directed a swift kick to Samuel's left leg. Samuel cried out and found *Don* Moisés standing over him, knife in hand, "I'm not finished with you."

As his assailant rode off, Samuel's mates helped him to his feet. His stance was unsteady, but this didn't prevent him from lunging over and punching one of his companions in the stomach. The man doubled over in pain while the other one backed away. Samuel limped over to the bench and gingerly lowered himself down while massaging his throat, "Thanks for nothing, you worthless bastards."

Several crates of trade goods were brought back from Kansas City that required immediate attention. Abran and Clemente unloaded the freight wagon at the store's rear entrance when they caught sight of *Don* Moisés. Strangely, he remained at a distance and motioned for Abran to approach. Clemente watched with great curiosity as Abran listened to his uncle. He bowed his head while running his fingers through his hair. An agitated Abran paced back and forth while kicking at a couple of rocks that were in his path. He turned to face *Don* Moisés and it appeared to Clemente that Abran was pleading with his uncle.

Suddenly, the elder Espinosa tried to urge his horse forward. An unfriendly exchange quickly ensued when Abran restrained his mount. Clemente approached his distraught companion a few seconds later when *Don* Moisés broke free and spurred his horse into action.

Father LaSalle was clearing some dead growth from a fenced garden plot when an unexpected apparition appeared in the form of *Don* Moisés approaching in a frenzied manner atop a sturdy chestnut horse. *Don* Moisés dismounted a few paces away and rushed over to confront him before the priest could react.

"I want the journal back, priest," shouted *Don* Moisés.

"You don't belong here, get out!"

Don Moisés was inches away from the priest's face, "Not until you return what belongs to me."

"I don't know what you are talking about, blasphemer."

Father LaSalle suddenly found the top part of his frock in *Don* Moisés' firm grasp. He struggled to escape.

"Liar! Samuel Ortiz confessed to me already."

"Release me! I know nothing of this accusation."

Don Moisés dragged the priest toward the rectory door and kicked the door open before shoving Father LaSalle inside, "Then let's have a look."

Father LaSalle smoothed his rumpled cassock and stretched out his right arm, "Be my guest, but I intend to file a complaint with the county constable."

"So do I you thieving -"

The sudden arrival of Abran and Clemente caught the priest and his accuser by surprise. Abran rushed up to restrain his uncle with his cousin's assistance, "*Tio*, please stop."

"Let go of me! I want him to return the journal."

Once Clemente had control of *Don* Moisés from behind, Abran stepped around and spoke in a hushed manner. "*Cuidado.* Please go outside with Cleme."

The calming presence of the younger males bolstered the pastor's valor, "Listen to your nephew. Your behavior only supports my claims about you."

Don Moisés nearly broke free from Clemente's clutches, which prompted Father LaSalle to retreat a step or two. "To hell with -," Abran interrupted his uncle's epithet by placing his hand over *Don* Moisés' mouth. He stepped closer and whispered, "Forgive me, uncle. Leave now. We'll take care of this another way. *¿Entiendes?*"

Abran's hand remained in place for a few tense seconds before *Don* Moisés nodded his head. Clemente coaxed him toward the door.

A contrite Abran faced Father LaSalle, "Please forgive this intrusion, Father. We'll help him find whatever he is looking for. Perhaps his housekeeper misplaced it."

"For the sake of your soul, I hope that you are not a conspirator in this mess."

Don Moisés lunged forward before being forced outside by Clemente, "Leave him alone! This feud is strictly between you and me."

Abran waited awhile before he spoke again, "Father, I'm sorry. My uncle can be an impulsive man, please forgive him."

"Have you been keeping our agreement, Abran?"

"Of course, Father."

"Then go. But make sure your uncle understands the severity of his actions."

"I will. Thank you."

Moments later, Father LaSalle peered out of the rectory door and observed Abran walking toward *Don* Moisés and Clemente in the church plaza. The three men stood in front of a freight wagon. For a moment, they briefly turned back toward the rectory which prompted the priest to pull his head back from the doorway. A few seconds later, Abran and Clemente boarded the wagon at the same time that *Don* Moisés mounted his horse. The trio rode away much to Father LaSalle's relief.

But *Don* Moisés audacity coupled with Samuel Ortiz's betrayal left him with a sense of dread that he had never felt before.

Chapter Seventeen

An influenza epidemic spread quickly through the Rio Sagrado valley which claimed many lives, particularly among the elderly and very young. On this particular night, Abran and Isabella faced their worst fears after Juan Pablo was stricken. A local *curandera*, a female healer skilled in the application of herbs and folk medicine, was summoned along with Father LaSalle.

Smoke from a bowl of smoldering herbs wafted toward a gathering of Espinosa and Lucero family members. The *curandera* prepared a poultice; *Doña* Nicolasa assisted her while a somber Isabella and *Doña* Maria stood nearby clutching their rosaries. *Don* Pablo and Abran entered the small bedroom and approached the crib.

Abran placed his hand on the child's forehead and addressed the healer, "He's burning up. Can't you do more?"

"I'm doing everything I can, *joven*. The rest is in God's hands."

Doña Nicolasa crossed herself as she placed her ear to the child's chest, "His breathing is getting weaker. When is Tomás going to get here with the *padre*?"

Isabella rushed over to her husband and buried her head in his chest. "Why does this have to happen? Juan Pablo is just a baby."

The sound of an opening door and familiar voices diverted everyone's attention. Father LaSalle walked in ahead of *Don* Tomás, while clutching a small black bag. A concerned *Doña* Maria, clinging to her Catholic ways, insisted that the priest be summoned should the Last Rites be needed; Abran and Isabella reluctantly consented mainly to maintain appearances. In truth, the sacrament's significance meant nothing to them. The older adults crossed themselves when the priest entered the bedroom.

Doña Nicolasa rushed to the arms of her husband then turned toward the priest, "It's the fever, *padre*. The baby is very weak."

The *curandera* bowed deferentially as Father LaSalle walked over to the crib. He placed his palm on the child's forehead and stooped down to listen to Juan Pablo's breathing. "I got here just in time."

The women broke into sobs of despair. The priest stepped toward a night stand, set the black bag down, and prepared to administer the Last Rites.

A short time later, Father LaSalle recited a prayer as the others watched helplessly. He reached for a small vial of oil, moistened his thumb, and traced the sign of the cross on the child's forehead. After moistening his thumb again, the priest turned to Isabella, "Could you undo his gown please?"

Isabella complied and watched as Father LaSalle anointed Juan Pablo's torso. The priest suddenly stopped his ritual; something unusual has caught his attention. He adjusted the gown ever so slightly and then queried the gathering in an outraged tone, "Why has this child been circumcised?"

A deliberate silence followed. Father LaSalle hastily removed his vestments and stuffed them into the bag. He turned to Abran, "You had this done during that trip, didn't you?" Abran stared back defiantly.

Doña Maria approached the enraged priest and pleaded, "Father, please finish the anointing! Juan Pablo is an innocent child. He doesn't deserve Purgatory."

As the priest continued speechlessly toward the door, *Don* Pablo rushed ahead to confront the priest. "You must go back and finish the Last Rites."

"Why should I?"

"Because you stand to lose this parish, you pompous fool," shouted *Don* Pablo

A haunting lament emanated from the small bedroom, followed by *Doña* Nicolasa's arrival.

"Juan Pablo is dead, our beautiful grandson is gone," she declared.

Don Tomás walked over and comforted his wife, while Abran bolted for the next room and cried out, "Isa."

Father LaSalle reached for the door latch – *Don* Pablo reacted by seizing his wrist. "Your days in this village are numbered. I will do whatever it takes to get rid of you."

"Move out of my way, señor! As it now stands, there will be no church funeral."

A reluctant *Don* Pablo released his grip, which allowed Father LaSalle to leave the premises. As he joined the other grieving relatives in the next room, *Don* Pablo began devising his scheme to have the spiteful pastor removed from their midst.

Chapter Eighteen

The disturbing correspondence from *Don* Pablo concerned Archbishop Lamy. In some respects, he expected something like this given Pierre LaSalle's officious nature. Now he was forced to deal with yet another unpleasant situation. The Archbishop knew enough to avoid underestimating the Espinosa's clout. Lamy envisioned the many empty pews along with the equally empty collection plates that reflected the sympathies of the Lucero and Espinosa clans as well as their close-knit *vecinos*.

I am writing your Excellency concerning a serious matter. When our village built the new church and rectory, we looked forward to a promising future. But now, the presence of Father LaSalle has become a problem. His contempt and lack of affection for the villagers is obvious. He has little respect for our way of life.

We can no longer tolerate this bitter, ungrateful man. We humbly request that Father LaSalle be removed from our parish immediately. Until this happens, we will withhold our financial support and attendance.

With all my respect,
Pablo Espinosa

Three hooded figures gathered one evening near a small barn belonging to Samuel Ortiz. After they dismounted from their horses, two of the men rounded up three steers and a saddle horse. The third man set down a lantern and piled hay in strategic piles. Before he set fire to the hay, *Don* Moisés inspected the steers' flanks by using the lantern for illumination.

"These belong to *Don* Sabino Leyba – they were stolen last week. Clemente, leave right away and return them. "

"*Si, patron.*"

Clemente turned to the other male before he rode off, "Be careful, Abran."

Abran gently slapped Clemente's horse on its right flank, "I'll see you later, Cleme."

The expanding fire cast an eerie glow as *Don* Moisés and Abran mounted their horses. "It's a pity that the other things have to burn. I'm sure the rightful owners would have wanted their possessions returned," observed Abran.

The barn was completely ablaze. *Don* Moisés and Abran retreated to a vantage point behind some bushes. A barking dog beckoned a drowsy Samuel and his wife, Celestina, outside. Dressed in a flannel nightshirt, Samuel raced for the barn and shouted out to no one in particular, "My horse, my tools!"

His wife followed him for a short distance and implored, "Come back, Samuel. It's too late."

Don Moisés and Abran watched as Samuel's silhouette raced up to the flames, his arms raised against the heat. Samuel fell to the ground and assumed a kneeling position before shouting out, "Who did this? Come out and show yourselves!"

Archbishop Lamy wasted little time in summoning Father LaSalle to his office. The two clerics faced each other two days after a messenger had been dispatched to Rio Sagrado. "This request from *Don* Pablo Espinosa disturbs me deeply, Pierre."

"Excellency, I can explain... "

"Not now. Your zeal is to be commended, but I wonder about your lack of compassion toward your flock."

Archbishop Lamy rose from his chair and paced behind his desk, "Your claims of Jewish practices within the Espinosa family may not be unfounded. But you are wrong in antagonizing *Don Pablo*."

"But the circumcision...," a disapproving look from his superior halted the priest's protest.

"Do you think you're the first of my pastors to be faced with this matter?"

Father LaSalle took a moment to process the Archbishop's revelation, "I suppose not."

"I've received similar reports of these Spanish Jews, but they pose no real threat to the Church."

"Perhaps we need to make examples of them."

"Why? We've already lost too many of our flock to the Presbyterians and Methodists. This would be a foolish move."

"But *Seigneurie*, there are none of those churches in Rio Sagrado."

"Not yet, Pierre, but that could change if we force our hand."

Archbishop Lamy motioned for Father LaSalle to join him in front of a large framed drawing. They studied an architectural rendering of the Romanesque-style Saint Francis of Assisi Cathedral being built in Santa Fe. It was based on the cathedral of Lamy's home diocese in Clermont-Ferrand, France, and he considered it a lasting representation of his work. The Archbishop said, "This spiritual center has been under construction for ten years now. My only hope for its completion depends on certain financial arrangements."

The priest diverted his gaze from the drawing to his superior.

"I have approached an influential Jewish businessman here in Santa Fe who seems willing to help out. This is a bad time for you to launch another Inquisition. Do you understand?"

Father LaSalle appeared lost in thought and returned to his seat. He turned toward Archbishop Lamy after a few moments,

"So you are removing me from Rio Sagrado?"

"Not necessarily. A lot depends on what you are willing to do."

That Saturday, a meeting took place at the Espinosa *hacienda*. Father LaSalle attempted to reason with *Don* Pablo, *Don* Tomás, *Doña* Maria, and *Doña* Nicolasa. *Don* Pablo, surrounded by his seated confederates, stood at the opposite end of a large table from the priest and spoke for the group. "Your apology is too late, Father. It won't undo the damage you have done."

"Please be reasonable, *señor*."

"I am being reasonable, as reasonable as you have been with us."

Doña Maria rose up to confront the priest, "Our grandchild's soul languishes in that wretched place because of your stubbornness."

Don Tomás joined the fray, "You went too far that night, *padre*."

"But we could make a new start. The first thing I would do is welcome *Señor* Espinosa back as the *mayordomo*."

"As far as I'm concerned, you and Samuel Ortiz deserve each other. Besides, we all know that the Archbishop put you up to this," responded *Don* Pablo.

"For the last time, I ask your forgiveness."

Doña Nicolasa startled everyone when she jumped up and pounded both of her fists onto the table, "Stop this! Forgiveness is something you have been lacking, Father. You have treated us disrespectfully ever since you arrived here. Worst of all, you preach to us about Christ's example, yet you fail to set such an example."

Don Tomás helped his distraught wife to her seat. *Doña* Maria crossed herself and appeared to recite a short prayer.

"Our position is final, *padre*. We will continue to withhold our support until a new priest is sent," affirmed *Don* Pablo.

The priest leaned on the table and bowed his head for several seconds. *Doña* Maria reached out for her husband's hand. Finally, Father LaSalle straightened up and clutched the crucifix hanging from his neck. "Very well, I will relay our conversation to His Excellency." He took a few steps toward the exit, but unexpectedly turned back to face his detractors. "But I will make sure that others know about the evil practices that take place in this village."

The priest stalked out of the patio before anyone could respond.

Chapter Nineteen

Abran came across Isabella as she sat on a wooden bench next to Juan Pablo's grave. Wildflowers were strewn on top of the burial mound. Dressed in a plain black dress, her face revealed a deep sadness as tears streamed down her cheeks.

Abran offered his hand to her, "Your sorrow concerns me, Isa. It touches everything around here."

Isabella accepted her husband's hand and rose from the bench.

"I can't help it. Juan Pablo was such a sweet child. He deserved a rich, full life," she cried out as she clung to Abran. Abran cupped Isabella's face in his hands and tenderly kissed her forehead. "You're right, Isa. But we weren't the only ones to lose a loved one from that fever."

Their lips met for several seconds. Abran escorted his wife toward the road that ran in front of their house. "Come walk with me for awhile."

Shortly after they departed, Abran stopped to pick a wildflower and offered it to Isabella. They continued their stroll after she kissed him on the cheek. Their attention was drawn to some sort of commotion in front of *Don* Pablo's house - a petulant Father LaSalle mounted his horse and rode away.

"It looks like we won't have to put up with him for very long, Isa. He better get the hell out of here if he knows what's good for him."

"Why do you say that?"

"You never know what might happen if he doesn't."

"*Callate, cariño.* Just pray that he leaves us soon."

Abran shouted in the direction of the priest. "Go back to France, *cabrón*!"

The couple resumed their walk, which concluded at a familiar spot - the tree grove near the river.

Abran drew Isabella near him. "Do you remember our secret meetings here?"

"I will never forget them, Abran."

"Do you remember when I talked about having lots of children?"

"Of course I do."

"And about the picnics that we'd have here with our screaming, noisy children?"

"I remember everything, *mi cariño*."

Tears welled up in Abran's eyes as he struggled to express his trepidation, "Do you still want more children even after...?"

Isabella placed a finger on Abran's lips and valiantly attempted to maintain her composure. Nodding her head, Isabella wrapped her arms around her husband's neck and released all the grief and uncertainty that had dwelt within her since Juan Pablo's death. Abran reached out and held her quaking body tightly against his for as long as she needed him to do so, which bonded their two spirits forever.

Chapter Twenty

I t didn't take long following the conclusion of Sunday Mass for word of Father LaSalle's foolish gambit to reach the Espinosa and Lucero families. Rather than accept his impending transfer diplomatically, the priest chose to publicize the Jewish presence within the village that set off a ruckus inside the church. One woman who was seated toward the front collapsed while shouting out a familiar exclamation. "*Dios mío!*"

Father LaSalle had mistakenly assumed that this revelation would rally many of the villagers to his cause and had assigned Samuel Ortiz the task of gathering signatures on his petition to the Archbishop. Despite Samuel's strategic location next to the exit, very few worshippers made an effort to sign the petition.

Father LaSalle's pompous frivolity would have made an amusing anecdote for the villagers to share for years to come had it not been for the next series of events.

The following day *Don* Moisés approached his house when a strange sight prompted him to a halt. A blackened object jutted over the top of a coal bucket that sat before the front door. Upon catching sight of its charred contents, a frantic *Don* Moisés overturned the container and rummaged through the burnt remnants of the journal. It was said that after clawing through the ashes, *Don* Moisés drew his blackened hands to his face and emitted an unsettling, mournful cry that could be heard for quite a distance. He refused to wash the soot from his face for several days afterward.

Early the next Sunday, Father LaSalle and Samuel Ortiz approached the sacristy with the intention of preparing for

Mass. They noticed the damaged lock on the sacristy door prior to entering the church. The suspicious priest immediately inspected the cabinets that contained his vestments and chalices while Samuel Ortiz opened the cupboard containing the communion wine and wafers.

"This is rather strange, everything seems in order. Did you notice anything missing?" asked the bewildered priest.

"Nothing's gone. Maybe the thief got scared."

Father LaSalle's query exposed his obvious mistrust, "Do you know of anyone who would try to steal from our church?"

"No, *padre*. That would be a mortal sin, right?"

Father LaSalle disregarded his *mayordomo's* gaffe and scanned the room once more. He checked the interior door that led to the altar just to be sure, but the intruder apparently ignored the passageway. "Let's get busy then," said the priest as he unlocked the door.

Later, the Celebration of the Eucharist was in progress when Father LaSalle drank from the chalice while reciting a muffled prayer in Latin. Soon the congregants knelt along the communion rail to receive the sacrament.

Just as Father LaSalle descended from the raised altar, he collapsed and rolled around on the floor while groaning loudly. Several women started screaming while a couple of men led by Samuel Ortiz rushed to the priest's side. Father LaSalle clutched his stomach as Samuel attempted to comfort him. The men quickly picked up the priest and carried him out of the church.

Several devout men and women organized a prayer vigil outside the rectory. One male, the *Hermano Mayor* or leader of the local *Penitentes*, led the rosary prayers interspersed with a dramatic narrative, while the others responded in a distinct, fast-paced manner. Soon, a man emerged from the rectory and headed directly into the church. Samuel Ortiz stepped out with a sorrowful look on his face. "Father LaSalle is dead. He went very fast."

Several of the women began to wail at the same moment that the church bell tolled in a protracted, somber fashion.

Father Bernard conducted the Funeral Mass two days later. Father LaSalle's body was laid to rest in a plot near the sacristy. The Archbishop's absence, along with many Espinosa and Lucero family members, was noticed by the villagers who attended the Mass and graveside service.

Following the funeral, Father Bernard asked Samuel and Celestina to gather up his friend's belongings. An open valise sat on the bed as Samuel opened the top drawer of a small bureau. He removed a book and deposited it into the valise before finding a gold pocket watch in the drawer. Samuel stuffed the watch into his pants pocket after he determined that it functioned properly. His wife stood in front of the kitchen table and was rinsing some cups in a small tub when Samuel entered carrying the valise.

"This should be the last of his belongings. Are you finished yet?"

"A few more minutes."

Samuel exited out the open rectory door. Celestina began to dry the cups when the creaking of the bedroom door startled her and set off a confusing sequence. As she turned toward the door, a gust of air rushed past her causing the door to slam shut followed by a cup smashing against the door.

Reacting to his wife's unearthly utterance, Samuel rushed back toward the rectory and was met at the door by his frantic wife. "Samuel, help me! Samuel!"

He placed his hands on her quivering shoulders and saw the terror in her eyes; it was a look that he never forgot. "What's wrong?"

"He's in there. He's come back."

"What are you talking about? Who's come back?"

"*El Padre*. His spirit is angry with us. Oh, *Dios mio!*"

Celestina buried her head in her husband's chest and began to cry uncontrollably.

Shortly afterwards, people claimed that the rectory was haunted by the spirit of Father LaSalle, though his name would be forgotten over time. They eventually referred to the apparition as the "ghost priest" and cited strange occurrences like locked doors being found ajar or articles being moved to adjoining rooms. Others mentioned the sensation of an unseen presence. After the rectory burned down at the turn of the century, several *viejitos* credited the vengeful "ghost priest" with this disaster.

Chapter Twenty-One

A few days later, Gregorio Lopez, the local constable, conferred with *Don* Pablo, *Don* Moisés, and Abran at *Don* Pablo's domicile. While seated around a large table in the patio, the four men shared a bottle of wine substantiating an air of informality amongst them.

"This matter of the priest's death is very puzzling you know," reported Gregorio.

"How is that, Gorio?" inquired *Don* Pablo, referencing his friend's childhood nickname.

"Samuel claims that Father LaSalle was poisoned. He didn't suspect anything until he realized that a bottle of communion wine was missing afterwards."

"How much faith do you put in that *cabrón's* word?" asked *Don* Moisés.

Gregorio smirked, "Not much usually, but the others at Sunday Mass are convinced that something suspicious happened."

"And I bet Samuel and his cronies suspect us, *verdad*?" added Abran.

The constable leaned forward with a concerned look, "It's my duty to look into all the possibilities. Your recent clashes with the priest are well known."

"What do you need from us, Gorio?" inquired *Don* Pablo.

"*Mira,* don't get me wrong, but I really need to know if any of you had a hand in the priest's strange death."

Abran rose from his chair and accidentally knocked over his goblet of wine. "This is ridiculous. Samuel Ortiz can go –"

"*¡Silencio!*" admonished *Don* Pablo.

"Yes father." Abran reached for his goblet as he returned to his seat.

"Please forgive my son's outburst, but his indignation should tell you everything you want to know. I can assure you that none of us would ever resort to such ridiculous measures."

Gregorio turned to the elder Espinosa. "*Don* Moisés?"

"Why would I risk losing everything just to be rid of that obnoxious priest? Besides, the Archbishop was going to remove him from Rio Sagrado."

The men paused momentarily while sipping some more wine. *Don* Pablo was the first to speak. "So are you convinced of our innocence in this matter?"

"*Si*. But I have to perform my duties, however unpleasant they may be at times."

"Don't apologize, Gorio. You're a damn good constable. That's why we keep electing you."

"*Gracias, Don* Pablo. I had better go now. I have report to the Archbishop by the end of the week."

The four men rose from their seats – the Espinosa males took turns shaking the constable's hand. *Don* Pablo extended a familiar farewell, "*Vaya con Dios.*"

Gregorio turned toward Abran while putting on his hat. "Give my best to Isabella and to *Don* Tomás and *Doña* Nicolasa. How is married life treating you?"

"Very well as you can see," responded Abran as he patted his stomach in an exaggerated manner.

They all shared a laugh before proceeding out of the patio together.

Two days later, Archbishop Lamy and Gregorio Lopez met in the Archbishop's office. After they had engaged in some informal chit-chat, the Archbishop gazed at an ornate crucifix hanging on a nearby wall before questioning the lawman.

"So what did your investigation uncover, Constable Lopez?"

"There are rumors that Father LaSalle was poisoned. But I couldn't find enough evidence to support that."

"So what do you think was the cause of death?"

"I really don't know. I'm sorry, Excellency."

"Perhaps God doesn't want us to know. I was in the process of removing Father LaSalle from his post. He abused his authority and alienated some important members of the community."

"Yes, Excellency. I was made aware of that during my investigation. Still, it's a shame that the *padre* is dead."

The Archbishop crossed himself and bowed his head for a moment – Constable Lopez followed suit. "May his soul rest in peace. To his credit, Father LaSalle was a superb administrator, but he failed to conform to his surroundings."

Gregorio hesitated before he continued his report, "There is another matter... forgive me."

The Archbishop noticed Gregorio's embarrassment. "What is it?"

"Some of the villagers claim that the rectory is haunted. Samuel Ortiz' wife swears that she was attacked by the priest's angry spirit."

The Archbishop's right palm slapped the desktop, which startled Gregorio. "Blessed Saint Francis, that's all I need now."

After staring up at the ceiling, the Archbishop returned his gaze to the lawman. "What do you think, Constable?"

"This has never happened to me before, Excellency. But I felt a definite chill during the time I was in the rectory."

"Sometimes our minds can deceive us at the oddest moments. Just stay strong in your faith and let's put this matter behind us. Have you told anyone else?"

"No one, not even my wife."

"Good, let's keep it that way. I'll ask Father LaSalle's successor to keep a close watch on things.

Archbishop Lamy stood up to indicate the meeting's conclusion. "I appreciate your time today, Constable Lopez. It sounds as if you did the best you could."

"Thank you, Excellency." Gregorio bowed while reaching for the Archbishop's hand. As he kissed the prelate's ring, the Archbishop muttered a blessing in Latin.

Chapter Twenty-Two

A gathering took place at the Lucero *hacienda* the following Sunday, the sumptuous meal was almost over when *Don* Tomás rose from his seat. "We are fortunate to be celebrating so many things today. First, the date has been set for Agapita and Clemente's wedding."

Don Tomás looked over at his blushing daughter who sat next to her betrothed. The attendees applauded politely. Abran and Isabella flanked Clemente; Abran rose from his seat and raised his goblet. "To my *cuñada* and my *primo*, may God grant you many happy years together. *¡Salud!*"

The attendees responded in unison, "*¡Salud!*"

"My daughter, Isabella, also wishes to make an announcement," added *Don* Tomás.

Isabella stood up and tugged on Abran's sleeves as he attempted to sit down. He rolled his eyes as he rose back up causing several of the celebrants to giggle. Isabella reached for Abran's hand before she spoke. "Abran and I are expecting our second child. Surprise!"

Doña Nicolasa and *Doña* Maria rushed over to Isabella. *Doña* Nicolasa kissed her daughter's hand. "*Hija*, this is wonderful news."

Doña Maria cradled Isabella's face in her hands. "God has answered my prayers."

Clemente offered a toast. "Enjoy the head start while you can. Agapita and I will soon catch up and pass you by. *¡Salud!*"

Don Tomás turned toward a particular person and held his hand out. "And finally, we welcome our new priest. His face is familiar to us. I think he will serve our parish well."

A hearty round of applause greeted Father Bernard as he rose from his seat. He politely addressed his host. *"Con tu permiso, Don* Tomás."

Don Tomás yielded the ceremonial stage to the priest. Father Bernard reached for a nearby wine bottle and filled his goblet. "I would like for all of you to join me." He waited patiently for everyone to ready themselves before he continued, "I want to thank you for your gracious hospitality this past week. I look forward to working with our *mayordomo, Don* Pablo."

Doña Maria turned admiringly to her husband as the attendees break into a lively cheer. Father Bernard waited for the celebration to subside before raising his goblet. *"Mis amigos,* to our wonderful, new fellowship..."

"¡Salud!" screamed everyone in attendance, as they lightheartedly completed the priest's token of affection.

There is a quarter-mile path that led from the church to the Rio Sagrado. After it passed over an *acequia,* a communal ditch used for irrigation, the trail followed a sloping fence line down to a small clearing that was used by certain men when they drank their cheap liquor. Occasionally one of them passed out overnight only to catch hell from his wife when he stumbled home the next day.

One morning, Juan Gonzales awoke to a bewildering apparition in the faint morning light. Fearing that someone had been sent to bring him home, the drunkard concealed himself behind a fallen cottonwood branch. An unrecognizable figure, unaware of the hidden presence, headed to the riverbank and removed a cork from a wine bottle. The shadowy figure tossed the wine bottle into the current after emptying the contents into the water. The drunkard's bloodshot eyes lingered too long on the floating bottle. By the time he remembered to look back, the specter has disappeared up the hill.

My grandmother told me of Juan Gonzales's dubious account of what he saw that morning. He claimed that the emptied wine bottle was the same one used by Father LaSalle that fateful Sunday morning. When questioned about the perpetrator's identity, he blamed the inadequate lighting or the nondescript clothing worn by the mysterious figure that made it impossible to determine the person's identity. It wasn't long before his friends resorted to tossing their empty bottles into the river and tormenting him with a derisive inquiry, "*¿Quien es, tonto, un fantasma o un hombre?*"

She also told me of the *viejitas* who gathered together to gossip about the priest's death. They spoke in their strange, hushed voices while concealing their faces under their black shawls. Some claimed that *Don* Moisés killed the priest out of revenge for the journal, while others blamed a distraught *Don* Pablo or an impetuous Abran. One *viejita* even alleged that Samuel Ortiz tried to frame his old enemy, *Don* Moisés.

I am thankful for the legacy that my grandmother's parents, Abran and Isabella Espinosa, chose to preserve and I can still hear my grandmother's voice reminding me of our heritage. "*Somos judíos, somos Sefardíes.*"

Epilogue

A few years ago, I made a pilgrimage to Spain to satisfy the curiosity that originated with my grandmother's astounding recollection. I lived out of my suitcase and a modern, air-conditioned bus for two weeks while touring the ancient cities of Toledo, Cordoba, Granada, and Sevilla. We visited the well-known landmarks like the Alhambra, walked the narrow alleys of the Santa Cruz Barrio, and frequented the countless, common tourist shops that marketed their overpriced souvenirs to an endless flow of *turistas*.

Cordoba, Sevilla, and Granada were dominant cities during the various Muslim dynasties that reigned from 711 to 1492, yet most remnants of the Sephardim have all but disappeared, save for an occasional restored synagogue. Gone are the centers of learning made possible because of the Muslim belief that a pluralism of cultures was not at war with the concept of an only God.

As a native New Mexican, I think of the times I have walked amongst the ruins of the long-deserted Native American villages. These were communities that existed about the same time as Spain's Golden Era. Holding a pottery shard in my fingers connects me to its creator. Touching a crumbling wall connects me to the villagers. If I listen closely enough, I might even hear the voices of the children playing or the communal chanting that blessed another successful harvest or hunting expedition.

When I touch the cold walls of the ancient synagogues or listen in vain for voices from the past, a profound sadness envelops my soul.

Glossary Of Main Characters

The following Espinosa ancestors recorded their thoughts in the old journal or preceded the story's inception:

Don Solomon de Espinosa – a prominent resident of Sevilla, Spain, who initiated the journal during the Expulsion Edict of 1492.

Alejandro de Espinosa – Solomon's grandson was the first Espinosa to leave for New Spain and established his mercantile operation in Zacatecas, Mexico in 1547.

Luis de Espinosa – departed for New Mexico in 1695 following Spain's repossession that followed the Pueblo Revolt of 1680 and helped found the village of Rio Sagrado.

Baltasar and Luisa Espinosa – the parents of Juan Antonio Espinosa.

Juan Antonio Espinosa – father of Moisés and Pablo who chose to conceal the family's Jewish past from his progeny.

The following are the elder members of the Espinosa, Lucero, and Valencia families ranging in age from 34 to 40 years. They all possessed fair complexions and mostly green- or blue-colored eyes reflecting their authentic Spanish heritage. The male physiques were sturdy, but shorter than their American contemporaries, topping 5-feet 6-inches. The women were four-to-six inches shorter with average-to-slim builds.

Pablo and Maria Espinosa – Abran's parents.

Tomás and Nicolasa Lucero – Isabella's parent.

Miguel and Emilia Valencia – Clemente's parents, Miguel and Maria are siblings.

Moisés Espinosa – Pablo's brother, twice a widower and childless, and Father LaSalle's antagonist.

These younger characters possessed the same attractive features as their parents and shared each other's secrets and predicaments:

Abran Espinosa – Isabella's beloved who sought to reclaim his Jewish birthright with his uncle Moisés.

Isabella Lucero – Abran's fiancé and eventual collaborator.

Clemente Valencia – Abran's cousin and trusted companion.

Agapita Lucero – Isabella's younger sister and Clemente's future bride.

Other prominent characters:

Jean Baptiste Lamy – the first bishop (1853) and archbishop (1875) of the Diocese of Santa Fe who retired in 1884.

Pierre LaSalle – French native and Rio Sagrado's first priest appointed by Archbishop Lamy.

Bernard Pitaval – Father LaSalle's friend going back to their French seminary days and second pastor of Rio Sagrado's church.

Isaac Cohen – the rabbi of Kansas City's first Jewish congregation and Don Moisés and Abran's spiritual advisor.

Samuel Ortiz – Father LaSalle's sycophant and a nemesis of the Espinosa family.

Celestina Ortiz – Samuel's wife.

Gregorio Lopez – Rio Sagrado's local constable.

Glossary Of Spanish Terms

Abuelito, abuelita – a term of affection spoken to a
  grandfather or grandmother.
Adios – goodbye.
Americanos – refers to an American, a recent arrival to
  New Mexico.
Andalé – hurry up.
Bizcochito – a cookie made with anise seed and coated
  with sugar and cinnamon.
Brujo, bruja – a warlock or witch.
Bueno – good.
Buenos dias – the greeting for "Good morning".
Burros – an unfavorable reference indicating that someone
  is stupid or oafish.
Bulto – a painted statue, usually carved from cottonwood
  branches and trunks.
Cabrón – an unflattering colloquial term meaning
  "bastard" (or worse).
Cállate! – Be quiet.
Cantina – a drinking establishment that might also serve
  food.
Chingadera – a crude slang term loosely interpreted as
  "screwed-up mess".
¿Cómo es posible? – how is this possible?
Compañero – a companion or trusted friend.
Con mucho gusto – with great pleasure.
Con tu permiso – a term requesting someone's permission
  or approval to speak.
Converso – a convert, sometimes referring to a Spanish
  Jew who converted to Catholicism and continued to
  practice his or her Jewish faith in secret.

Cuidado – be careful.

Cuñada – sister-in-law.

Desgraciado – an unflattering term meaning "miserable wretch".

Dios mío – My God.

Don, Doña – used a term of respect for a prominent male or female of the community.

El Día Grande – The Great Day, a crypto-Jewish term for Yom Kippur.

Entremetido – a meddler or busybody.

Español(es) – a Spaniard or Spaniards.

¿Estás listo? – are you ready?

Fiesta – a celebration or festival.

Gracias – thank you.

Gringo – a less flattering term for a Yankee or American.

Hacienda –a large family home or ranch house.

Hermano – brother.

Hija, hijo – daughter, son.

Hija mía – my daughter, an affectionate term used by a parent while talking to a child.

Hombre – man.

¿Entiendes? – do you understand?

Joven – a young person.

La Iglesia de San Ysidro – The San Ysidro Church.

La Paloma – the dove.

Lámbe – an unflattering term referring to a sycophant or toady.

Malcriado – an ill-bred or impolite person.

Mañana - morning or tomorrow morning.

Mantilla – a decorative shawl usually placed over a woman's head.

Mayordomo – a person who assisted the priest with important parish matters.

Mestizo – the New World descendants of Spanish and indigenous parents.

Mí cariño – my dear or my love.
Mira – look.
Mís amigos – my friends.
Nuevo Mexicanos – citizens of New Mexico.
Padre – priest or father.
Para mís vecinos – for my neighbors.
Patrón – an employer or powerful person within the
    community.
Por favor – please.
Primo – cousin.
Qué bonita – how pretty.
¿Qué no? – don't you think?
¿Quién es, tonto, un fantasma o un hombre? – Who is it,
    fool, a ghost or a man?
¿Quién sabe? – Who knows?
Salud – a wish for someone's well-being that is extended
    while drinking wine or spirits.
Señor, señora – mister, misses.
Sí – yes.
Silencio – a stern command for silence.
Sobrino – nephew.
Somos judíos – we are Jews.
Te amo – I love you.
Tío – uncle.
Válgame Dios – Bless me.
Vamanos! – let's go.
Vaquero – cowhand or cowboy.
Vaya con Dios! – go with God or God be with you.
Vecino – neighbor.
Verdad – the truth or true.
Viejito, viejita – an affectionate term referring to an older
    man or woman.
Y todos los santos – "and all the saints".

Paternal Grandparents
Jose Antonio and Maria Emilia (Mares) Martinez

Maternal Grandparents
Ines and Anna Maria (Lucero) Valencia

Published with support from

Institute for Tolerance Studies
a 501 c 3 organization that does research, publications,
workshops, and conferences on social justice and conflict
resolution, addressing issues ranging from ethnicity to religion, language, gender, and freedom of speech.

LaVergne, TN USA
28 September 2009
159178LV00001B/114/P